I0625064

THE IMPETUOUS HEIRESS

BY ALINA K. FIELD

Copyright © 2021 Mary J. Kozlowski
ISBN No. 978-1-944063-368
Havenlock Press
PO Box 1891
La Mirada, CA 90637-1891

March 1, 2022
Previously Published in the *Christmas Kisses Regency Holiday Romance Anthology*, October 12, 2021

This is a work of fiction. Names, characters, places, and incidents either are the product of the author's imagination or are used fictitiously, and any resemblance to actual persons, living or dead, business establishments, events, or locales is entirely coincidental.

All rights reserved under International and Pan-American Copyright Conventions. No part of this text may be reproduced, transmitted, downloaded, decompiled, reverse engineered, or stored in or introduced into any information storage and retrieval system, in any form or by any means, whether electronic or mechanical, now known or hereinafter invented without the express written permission of the copyright owner, except in the case of brief quotations embodied in critical articles and reviews.

The reverse engineering, uploading, and/or distributing of this book via the internet or via any other means without the permission of the copyright owner is illegal and punishable by law. Please purchase only authorized editions, and do not participate in or encourage electronic piracy of copyrighted materials. Your support of the author's rights is appreciated.

Cover Design by Dar Albert

When dashing Fitzhenry Lovelace escorted sensible Mary Elizabeth (Mel) Parker to a once in a lifetime meeting with her estranged grandfather, an unexpected romance bloomed that had nothing to do with the old man's immense wealth. Throwing caution to the wind, she said a wholehearted yes to Fitz. But before they could finalize their nuptials, a family emergency called Fitz away. Then he stopped answering her letters.

Months pass and the Yuletide arrives, and Mel faces the fact that her impetuosity has led to a Dilemma. Worse, word arrives that her ruthless mother is descending upon her with a horrid replacement for Fitz in tow. But when Mel bolts, her meddling cousin plans an unexpected stop on the journey.

Having made a hash of his finances and neglected Mel, Fitz realizes he must make amends with the woman he still loves. But before he can act, she arrives on his doorstep. He soon senses more is amiss with her than just his careless courtship. Can he uncover her secrets and win her back before he loses her altogether?

Originally published in the
*Christmas Kisses
Regency Holiday Romance Anthology*

CHAPTER ONE

What About Him?

25 September, 1822

The Sawley Estate, Bedfordshire

"No, no, no, Mary Elizabeth." Gregory Sawley's cane hit the floor with each *no*, though the thick Turkey carpet rather muffled the dramatic effect. "It is not enough for you to have a knowledge about markets, compounding interest, and commodity futures, *and* a dependable stock jobber. The key is to have access to reliable information. The key is for you to make a *proper* marriage."

Heavens.

"Marriage, sir?" Mary Elizabeth Parker—Mel to her late father and her cousin, Hermione—took in a quelling breath. "And hand over my inheritance to a nodcock of a husband who'll dismiss all my ideas?"

She pressed her lips closed on an even sharper retort. If she wanted to be nagged and prodded about matrimony, she might have remained at

Lady Clitheroe's house party for today's activity, a picnic, with her much older widowed cousin, Lady Hermione Gravelston and the other guests.

Hermione had wangled their invitations to the Michaelmas marriage mart Lady Clitheroe was hosting, convinced that at five-and-twenty, there was still hope for Mel. For her part, she'd been glad to attend, but not for the purpose of meeting marriageable men. She'd escaped this day for the once in a lifetime chance to visit one of Lady Clitheroe's not-too-distant neighbors, one of England's most successful bankers, Gregory Sawley. Her grandfather.

After the solicitor managing her money bungled an investment, she'd decided that if her grandfather could rise from humble beginnings to become as rich as Croesus, she ought to be able to manage her own small inheritance herself. She had a plan, and it didn't include matrimony, a risky endeavor even in the most optimistic of circumstances. After months of exchanging letters with her grandfather, she'd jumped at the chance to meet him and be tutored in person.

And he'd been altogether welcoming this day. He'd answered all her questions, and provided a very good luncheon, and then, having more to say, he'd escorted them to his expansive library. Two fireplaces, one at each end, warmed the room against the autumn chill. Above the nearby mantel, the late Mrs. Sawley, Mel's grandmother, gazed lovingly at the golden-haired babe on her lap, the child who would grow up to be Mel's headstrong mother. Amazingly, the artist had caught the willfulness in the wide blue eyes and bowed lips of his younger subject.

Outside, the day was advancing, heavy clouds obscuring the late afternoon sun. If they didn't leave soon, they might have to stay the night.

Was that why her grandfather had required this parting lecture? Did he want her to stay? Pain lurked in his eyes, and his gray pallor and gaunt frame belied the strong voice, putting her in mind of her father's last illness. She might never see him again, and though their acquaintance was short, she'd miss him, as she still grieved for her father, dead these two years.

"I said a proper marriage, one with proper contracts and settlements, to a man in the Commons, or a lord would do. Your stepfather likely has contacts, but you will not want to be under his thumb, I think."

A shiver went through her. Upon Papa's death, she'd dodged that *thumb*, and Mother's broad hints at a betrothal to her stepfather's nephew. She'd fled to Hermione in Hampshire while her mother returned to her husband-to-be in Kent. And the man her mother married would be no help at all to her financial plans. He was far too indolent to take up his seat in the Lords. He'd be nothing but her mother's tool, and an utter hindrance.

"Aren't such men often rather pompous and foolish, sir?"

Across the room, a throat cleared loudly.

Grandfather's lips quirked and he tipped his head toward the interruption. "What about him?"

The *him* in question was seated on the far end of Grandfather's spacious library, and apparently had perfect hearing.

Oh, he met Grandfather's requirements in some ways. He had a seat in the Commons, and someday he would inherit and move on to the

Lords. He was also unmarried, his wife having died in childbirth the previous year.

And breathtakingly handsome with rumpled golden hair, soulful blue eyes, and a wide-shouldered, narrow-hipped, long-limbed form that had at first sight sent her blood pounding. Fortunately, she'd had many years following the drum with Papa, and had seen enough well-formed men to master her baser urges.

She shook her head. "It is not that way between us, sir. In truth, I'm rescuing him today from marriage-minded mamas and their daughters."

"What way must it be? You are a female. Your financial plans require social connections, ones that in your case can only be achieved by marriage. If you don't believe me, ask Mr. Lovelace."

Grandfather pointed the tip of his cane at the overstuffed wing chair placed near the opposite fireplace. Mr. Fitzhenry Lovelace, eldest son and heir of Baron Loughton, had retreated there and waited at his ease, allowing them a modicum of privacy whilst imbibing every word.

Mr. Lovelace wasn't likely to agree with Grandfather on this subject, having that morning accosted her in Lady Clitheroe's stables, begging the honor of conveying her here in order to escape two doe-eyed misses vying to be the first to be compromised by him.

Mel squeezed her hands together to prevent them from rubbing at the ache between her eyes. After forcing his presence upon her today, Lovelace might as well come and defend her desire to remain unmarried. "What say you, Mr. Lovelace?" she called.

He put aside his book and stood.

Grandfather waved him over, directing him to the sofa where she sat.

She slid to one end, and he seated himself at the other. "Well?" she asked.

"My father always says, it helps to know what is not in the newspapers."

The deep, melodious tones made her skin tingle and her cheeks warm. Unlike some handsome men, Mr. Lovelace's appeal didn't diminish when he opened his mouth. They'd been seated much closer when they chatted in the phaeton, but the cool morning air had provided a good excuse for her blushing. Plus, there'd been no one to study her as her grandfather was now doing.

Lovelace stretched his muscular legs and crossed them at the ankles. "A word dropped at the club, in the coffee room of Parliament, or on the grouse field can be useful. Or not."

"I know your father." The cane *thunked*, more gently this time. "A wise and prudent man. Rather too many children one might say. You are the eldest of..."

"Ten. Six boys and four girls."

Envy settled over Mel, and she glanced up at the portrait again. She'd longed for brothers or sisters, but eventually had realized the production of siblings required a husband and wife who tolerated each other. Unlike her parents. After their imprudent elopement and the birth of their daughter, Major and Mrs. Parker had gone their separate ways even during the times when they resided under the same roof.

"Mary Elizabeth, observe that Mr. Lovelace's father, Lord Loughton, has managed to build prosperity for himself and his children by his engagement in politics and trade, something you cannot yourself do. But you do have common sense."

Unlike your mother. His pained look communicated that message.

"You must marry the right sort of man if you wish to acquire the contacts and information needed to grow the bequest Parker left you...how much was it?"

Her father hadn't been wealthy, but he wasn't a pauper either. He'd left a small income for Mama, in spite of their estrangement and her abandonment, in spite of knowing that the moment he drew his last breath she'd marry her lover. He'd left a previously unknown cottage in Durham and the rest of his wealth and worldly goods to Mel. She should be able to live comfortably with a housemaid or two. She wasn't greedy for more, not really. She relished the challenge of making her own future.

He *thunked* the floor again. "How much, Mary Elizabeth?"

She'd never shared that detail with her grandfather before, but she did so now.

Grandfather's lips pressed together. Any discussion of Papa, who'd stolen away his only child without permission, was painful to him. Clearly, Mother's failure to make an approved marriage still weighed on Gregory Sawley's mind.

"It is more than adequate for my needs." She didn't need Grandfather's fortune. In fact, the thought of managing it was frightening. The money would be a magnet for fortune hunters and leeches, anxious to get their hands on it for their grouse fields, stables, and dilapidated castles. Before he died, Papa had reminded her to be careful, for even her small income could draw a bounder who might take her inheritance and, in his words, *piss it against the wall.*

"I will tell you again, Grandfather, I'm not here to wheedle you for money. I'm grateful for your wise counsel." *Mostly wise, except for this last business about marrying.* "I accept your decision on the matter of your estate and I fully intend to take care of myself."

After a long look, he harumphed. "I will double what he's left you and add it to his bequest, else you'll only have beef on the holidays. Smith." He signaled a specter seated at a desk in the far corner, scribbling.

Likely recording their every word. Grandfather was that sort.

"Make a note of that, Smith. Now, my joints are telling me that the weather is turning. You'd best get back on the road."

As she'd suggested to him earlier. Mel stood and took the old man's hand. It was skin over bone, and the touch sent her emotions tumbling. Papa was lost to her, and this man was the only one left in her life.

But his presence in her life was new and, even if he lived many more years, tenuous, and she must remember that. He had disowned his own daughter for her marriage, and Mel was the product of that imprudent union.

"Thank you for your time today, Grandfather. If ever I am able, may I come to visit you again?"

"If you are able, if I am able, yes."

His squeeze on her hand sent tears to her eyes. Which she promptly blinked back, wishing him a good day and walking purposefully to the door while Mr. Lovelace said his own farewell and followed.

CHAPTER TWO

A Visit to an Old Friend

Friday, 27 December, 1822
Loughton Manor, Leicestershire

Fitzhenry Lovelace, Lord Loughton, accompanied his younger brother George and George's fiancée, Sophie, Lady Glanford, out of the front door of Loughton Manor into the overcast chill. The traveling chaise awaited, baggage stowed and horses snorting and blowing ice crystals.

Their mother, Lady Neda Loughton, hurried out to say her farewells, tugging a shawl around her before kissing both Sophie and George.

"Safe travels, Sophie," Fitz said, squeezing her hand. "Your boys will be well cared for while you're gone. I promise."

She sent him a long look and finally nodded. "I'm counting on it, Fitz."

George handed her into the chaise and turned back to grasp Fitz's shoulders. "Good luck with the other matter, Brother." He kissed Mother one more time, then climbed in and could be seen tucking a rug up to his lady's chin as they pulled away.

"What other matter?" Concern etched the corners of Mother's bright blue eyes.

He put an arm around her and escorted her into the parlor where a fire had been lit, and she turned to face him. "What other matter?"

"The matter of Miss Parker."

She bit her lip. "Do not tell me you intend to break with her. The banns have been called, and they're not yet void."

He helped her into a chair near the hearth and stood facing the fire. "I must give her the option. I must tell her the truth." The truth that, between bad investments, bad crops, and some very bad loans, he'd bungled the family finances. That the lady who'd never resided in luxury would still have to pinch pennies if she went through with their marriage.

Mother appeared next to him and her soft hand settled upon his cheek. "Do you care for her, Fitz?"

He thought of Miss Parker's dark, intelligent eyes, and her determination to take care of herself, and her kindness, even while saying exactly what she thought.

Yes, most certainly he cared for her. And he missed her. He hadn't seen her since late September, and the intervening months had been filled with Father's illness and death, his desperate attempts to untangle the mess he'd made, and other dark news. He'd let down his father, his family, and his new fiancée.

She was so unlike Alice, his first wife. Their union had been an inevitability, one he'd finally agreed to with some optimism. After all, his parents had fallen into that sort of marriage and true love and partnership had grown between them. Unfortunately, with Alice, long acquaintance and optimism hadn't produced marital bliss. Far from it.

"Your father's illness and death unsettled us all. I never told you, but I confess, it seemed a hasty engagement so soon after Alice's death."

After a mere ten days acquaintance with Miss Parker, he'd tumbled into an engagement that hadn't seemed the least bit impulsive.

"There'd been something of an impropriety. When I drove her to visit her grandfather, we were quite late returning to the house party because of a rainstorm. We stopped at an inn until the storm abated and shared a private dining room."

She eyed him closely. "And that is all?"

"We talked. Quite a lot."

She raised an eyebrow.

"I kissed her hand." He smiled, remembering. He'd kissed the palm of Mel's ungloved hand, raising the devil of a blush on her creamy cheeks. Mother didn't need to know that. "No kissing on the lips." That had come later.

"Well. From what you describe, it was an impropriety you both might have weathered."

They might have. Mel was an on-the-shelf spinster who claimed no interest in matrimony and he was a widower. They'd merely spent a full day together from early morning to near midnight, but that interval had allowed him to know Mel Parker. He'd jumped at the chance to spend the rest of his life with her.

Oh, but there'd been so much deuced dark news since.

"I'll ask again, do you care for her?"

He lifted her hand away from his cheek and held it. "I do. As I said, we did much talking." Far more than he ever did with Alice. "And I must see her, Mother. I spent last night rereading her letters." Chatty letters about her journey home and the stock market had devolved into ones fretting about the health of her grandfather after his stroke, and then chiding letters asking about the plans for their future. Some had been misdirected; some he hadn't seen until his return Christmas Eve. He'd always replied to the ones he'd received, though he was never one to write a tome.

In her letter dated the second week of December she informed him that she would not write again until she heard back from him. He'd been in London, and then had gone directly to Enderby for a prearranged visit to see a friend's agricultural improvements. He'd only just seen her note.

"Can you manage the boys, Mother? Would you mind awfully if I miss seeing the New Year in with the family? I must travel to Hampshire and speak with Miss Parker in person. A letter will not do."

She turned her gaze to the burning coals for a long pause, finally nodding. "Yes, you must settle matters with her. Today, though, I'd ask you to visit old Sarah. I was planning to deliver her Christmas basket myself, but with the weather and the children..."

"I'd be happy to, Mother." Their old nurse had retired to a cottage in a neighboring village. The errand would take him away until at least the late afternoon, and he'd have time to think.

"There have also been some problems with the Cruikworks," she said, "but I'll ask the vicar to pay them a call."

Jem Cruikwork was the son of a longtime tenant, who'd returned from the war with a lingering injury and a troublesome bride. "Jilly and Jem are going at it hammer and tongs again?"

"Something like that." She glanced at her timepiece. "You have time to take breakfast with the boys and Nancy, and then you must away and make haste to return before dinner." She took his arm and escorted him to the breakfast room, a spring in her step, and a smile on her lips.

Mother hadn't smiled so spontaneously since before Father's death, and she wasn't at all displeased he would miss seeing in the New Year. What was she up to?

Mel held her last clean handkerchief to her nose and tried to gulp down the small piece of toast she'd nibbled at the last inn.

"We have almost arrived, dear heart." Lady Hermione Gravelston held the bucket they'd acquired several days earlier at the Crown and Rose, where they'd made the first stop on this journey.

The traveling chaise was a small one with good visibility all around. Hermione's ample form, squeezed up next to Mel, cushioned some of the bumps. And instead of a rollicking bone-shaking gallop, the icy wet weather had kept the horses to a pace that accommodated Mel's affliction. She'd had a full two nights and a day of rest, spending Christmas in a Northamptonshire inn, yet still her stomach refused to cooperate.

She squeezed her eyes shut on the sight of a prosperous village, praying they would soon stop for a change of horses, or, though it was still early, for the night. When she opened them, they were passing an inn with a swinging sign displaying a crowned swan.

"We're not stopping there?" she cried.

Hermione did more of her annoying patting. "No, dear one. It will only be a tiny bit farther."

"That looked to be a respectable posting inn. I cannot imagine we can find anything better in this part of Leicestershire and... *oh*."

The chaise had hit yet another bump. Mel clutched the bucket and retched so prodigiously she expected to see part of her insides in the bottom.

"I cannot... I cannot go on like this."

"Only a little farther. We're almost there."

They approached a break in the boundary wall of a private estate and the postboy looked back. Hermione nodded and waved, and the horses turned onto the muddy drive, passing between low drifts of melting snow.

"This is someone's home," Mel said.

"I wrote to a friend about our journey, and when I told her we would be traveling this way, she insisted we stop and visit. After all, we were only in a hurry to depart, but it doesn't matter if our arrival in Durham is delayed."

"But...but, Cousin, it's the Yuletide. Will we not be inconveniencing the family?"

"Not at all."

The coach wobbled at a turn and another unsettling wave assaulted her. She closed her eyes a moment, holding her breath.

When she opened them, they had arrived at a grand manor house. A groom, a liveried footman, and a stately older man, who had to be the butler, appeared.

An uneasy feeling came over her, one not related to the nausea afflicting her. She had wanted to join the Great North Road in London, but Hermione had argued that this route through the Midlands would throw off their pursuers. Unfortunately, they were passing through Leicestershire, the home of her erstwhile fiancé.

"Who is this friend, Hermione?"

"Lady Neda. You will like her. I haven't seen her in years, but we had our come-out together."

"Lady Neda who?"

The footman opened Hermione's door, and her cousin beamed at the handsome young man, ignoring Mel completely.

The groom appeared on her side, standing ready to help her.

She handed him the bucket and climbed out. "I'm so sorry, but will you see to this?" She couldn't very well take it in, and she didn't want to leave it bouncing out its contents inside the chaise as the it headed off to the posting inn.

He blinked and took the bucket, stepping away.

"Wait," she said. "Whose home is this?"

He blinked again. The servants would think her mad—well she was, wasn't she? She'd made a hash of her life during the last few weeks. Weepy, and sick, and waspish, she wasn't herself at all. And this last desperate escape avoiding Mother's arrival...

"This is Loughton Manor," he said.

Hades. Her stomach lurched again when it should know very well there was nothing left to cast up. She steadied herself against the side of the chaise.

The groom put aside the bucket. "May I help you, miss?"

She waved him away. "I will be fine," she said through the wadded handkerchief.

Visiting an old friend, indeed. Hermione had tricked her. No wonder she'd been so accommodating about their hurried departure from Hampshire.

"Mel." Hermione touched her arm. "Do not worry."

"How *could* you?" Maybe she could climb in and have the postilion convey her to that very respectable inn. She might crawl into a bed and stay there until her traitorous cousin had finished her visit. Perhaps she'd grown into a coward since late September.

Oh, very well, she had. And she was ill, too ill for a confrontation. And there were servants hovering around, unloading their trunks, chatting to the postilion, all available to witness her abject humiliation.

"I have it on good authority that Lord Loughton is away at a hunting party," Hermione whispered back.

Of course, he was. It seemed he spent most of his time away at house parties and hunts.

"Come along now. You'll feel better inside. We'll make you some ginger tea."

Her cousin linked arms with her, and they watched the chaise pull away, returning down the lane.

"One night's stay, Hermione. We must leave on the morrow, without delay. Mother may have already landed in England. And this break in the weather may not hold." Mel drew in a breath. "I shall claim illness and go straight to bed and stay there for the duration."

"No. You've done far too much of that already."

Mel bit back an oath, though she couldn't deny it was true. She'd spent too many days whining and worrying. Why, Papa would turn in his grave at seeing her acting so ninny-headed. She'd resolved to pull herself together, and she would. Before her unexpected engagement, she'd had a plan: live simply, manage her investments, and remain happily unmarried. And now, she would follow it through. Fitzhenry Lovelace could go to the devil.

She didn't want to marry *him* either.

"Perhaps his mother will convey to him that we are no longer engaged."

"Would it not be better to force his hand? He's a matrimonial prize."

And *she* was not, as everyone with eyes in their head and a knowledge of financial gossip knew. Fitzhenry Lovelace, Lord Loughton now, was too handsome, too rich, and too utterly desirable for the likes of Mary Elizabeth Parker. Which was why his replies to her letters were brief and impersonal, when he bothered to answer at all. It was galling to be ignored, especially when one wasn't feeling well.

"Why settle for a matrimonial prize when I might someday have a chance at love?" She had no intention of marrying, but talk of love matches always placated Hermione, who missed her late husband terribly.

"You are certain this is not love?"

It had been for her, or so she'd thought. Not at first meeting, of course—Fitz had merely stirred her carnal interest then, being a fine specimen of a man.

But the day she'd spent with him traveling back and forth to her grandfather's and sheltering from the rain at an inn for a few hours had provided a chance to know him. He had the unusual ability to listen, and he was honest about his limitations. His father and brothers were better at financial management than he was. He claimed having a clever wife wouldn't intimidate him. By the time they arrived at Lady Clitheroe's that night, she was well on the way to being head over ears in love with him.

Though she'd never expected it, he'd returned her regard, at least until the terrible news of his father's illness arrived and he left her to rush home, after which he didn't. His letters petered off until he finally stopped writing altogether. If this was love, then clearly, love wasn't enough.

"It doesn't matter. I'm setting him free."

"He'll need to woo you again."

"It won't work." She wouldn't be fooled twice.

They crossed the wet drive and reached the bottom step of the portico when a woman appeared in the doorway. "Lady Hermione." Clutching her shawl, she stepped out and grasped Hermione's forearms. Almost a hug, quite a strong gesture of endearment for a friend one hadn't seen in decades, a friend Mel had known nothing about. The two women exchanged enthusiastic greetings and Hermione made introductions.

The lady turned a warm smile up to Mel. "Miss Parker. It is such a pleasure to make your acquaintance."

She was a pixie, a fairy: petite, golden-haired under her lacy cap, her blue eyes filled with what appeared to be genuine kindness.

"Lady Loughton." Mel managed a wobbly curtsy. "We are surely inconveniencing you, appearing so suddenly."

Lady Loughton blinked, slid a gaze to Hermione, and then beamed another smile that wrapped around Mel like a warm blanket. "Not at all. Do come in and sit by the hearth while the servants light the fires in your bedchambers."

The open doors of a large parlor flanked the hall, but Lady Loughton led them up the stairs to a more intimate sitting room that perhaps adjoined her bedchamber. Before they could seat themselves, servants arrived with tea and a tray of food, and Lady Loughton set about pouring.

Mel accepted her saucer and cup carefully and inhaled. Now that she was out of the bouncing chaise, her stomach had settled enough that she could at least attempt to taste it. She sipped and then reached for a biscuit.

"Mel is not a good traveler," Hermione said. "She has been casting up her accounts since we left Hampshire."

"I am feeling better now."

"Mel?" Lady Loughton asked.

"Short for Mary Elizabeth," her cousin said.

"You must ask the servants for anything you think will ease your discomfort," Lady Loughton said.

A carriage that would carry her away from here would do.

"If you hear shouting and pounding feet, that will be the boys. I do hope they won't disturb you. And I'm sorry Fitz isn't here to welcome you. He'll be so happy to see you tonight."

She spluttered and dabbed at her mouth. *Tonight?* Hermione had lied.

"Is he not away, Lady Neda?" Hermione asked, all innocence.

"Only for the afternoon. He's gone to deliver a basket to one of our pensioners who's been ill."

Mel's hand shook, tea sloshing over the rim of the cup and onto her carriage dress. She glared at her cousin and mopped at the spill. "He's not away hunting?"

"He was, but his brother, George, fetched him home on Christmas Eve. George has just become engaged to Sophie, Lady Glanford. He and Sophie left for London today to see to some business, but they'll return before Twelfth Night and be married in our parish church. I hope you will stay and attend."

A wedding.

Mel's vision clouded, her ankles and feet tingled, and black dots appeared on Lady Loughton's pale face and white cap.

"Miss Parker?" Her cup disappeared and a hand touched her shoulder.

"Bend over and take deep breaths." Hermione's raspy voice came from a distance.

Mel squeezed the top of her nose between her brows and shook her head. "I am fine."

Lady Loughton moved closer on the sofa. "You must have a rest before dinner. My younger children will be joining us, and Lady Glanford's two boys, and of course, Fitz. You will get to meet everybody."

The lady's excitement was palpable—and she was destined to be disappointed. Mel couldn't let this farce continue.

"This... this is a mistake, ma'am." She angled herself to face both the lady next to her and her traitorous cousin seated in a chair just beyond. "I should tell you that I had no part in planning this visit, imposing on you at Christmas, forcing myself upon...upon... You are mistaken about your son. He will not be the least bit happy to see me."

Her voice shook. She took in a breath, willing herself not to weep. There'd been enough weeping. Blast it all, what would Papa say if he could see her acting like this? What would Grandfather say?

She was acting just like Mother, and that would not do.

She sat up taller. "I appreciate your kindness and your hospitality, but I am quite frankly *mortified* to be here. In fact, I should be more than happy to remove myself to the nearby inn while you and my cousin visit."

A long pause ensued during which she focused on the pink roses gracing the china service.

"Mel," Hermione cautioned.

The pixie next to Mel remained still. She chanced a glance at Lady Loughton and saw her studying the same china pot. Perhaps there were answers in the tea leaves.

Mel's hands twisted together in her lap. "You must think me rude after you have been so kind, and I suppose I am."

The door flew open. "*Grandmama*," a child cried.

Glad for the interruption, Mel glanced over her shoulder and saw two urchins, a dark-haired boy and a little girl with hair as golden as Lady Loughton's. Both of them had pulled up and halted, surprised by the presence of visitors.

Lady Loughton beckoned. "Come, Mary, Ben. We have guests."

The little girl approached, the boy following. She curtsied; he bowed.

"This young man is Benjamin Halverton, Lady Glanford's younger son. And this young lady is Mary Lovelace, Fitz's daughter."

Mary. Mel pressed a hand to her waist. Fitz had told her about his daughter, but she'd never learned the little girl's name.

Oh, Hades, she hadn't bothered to ask him for it. It was just as well she was breaking the engagement. What a poor excuse for a stepmother she would be.

The little girl approached and clung to her grandmother's knees, her blue gaze studying Mel. The little boy's attention had shifted to the tray of biscuits.

Intelligence flickered in those bright blue eyes; intelligence, interest, and a hint of worry.

She knows, Mel thought. *Was it possible? Might Fitz have told her?*

"My name is Mary also," she said. "I am Mary Elizabeth. Do you have a middle name?"

The girl gave her a smile that could break hearts, revealing a full set of delicate white teeth. "I am Mary Anastasia."

Warmth flooded her. This was a precious child, polite, well-mannered, and soft-spoken, and she might have been hers to love—a stepchild of course, but what of that? Her own cousin Hermione was more of a mother to Mel. "That is a beautiful name."

"Children, this is Lady Hermione and Miss Parker, and you may each take one biscuit, but don't spoil your appetite for dinner."

"I'm so sorry, my lady." An older woman spoke from the doorway, her cap askew, her expression harried. "Miss Nancy was to watch them. I can't find her, but I've gathered the boys and got them back upstairs. Tilly will take these two back to the nursery."

A much younger servant appeared in the doorway, little more than a child herself.

"Go along with Tilly, then," Lady Loughton said.

Benjamin stalled, eying the platter, his lips lined with crumbs, while Mary dawdled over to her grandmother, reaching up to her for a hug and evoking a fond smile from the older lady.

Mel wanted to laugh at the obvious foot-dragging. She would have if her insides weren't still rumbling.

"There now," Lady Loughton said, with a final kiss. "Off you go."

Instead of complying, Mary curtsied to Hermione, and then turned those astonishing blue eyes on Mel.

The child stood in front of her grandmother, close enough for Mel to reach out to her. And she did, her hands and arms working of their own accord.

It was confusing and...and...instinctive. But nevertheless, preposterous, and probably a mistake. She liked children, enjoyed their exuberance even, but she wasn't marrying this darling girl's father.

The scent of soap rose around tangled blonde curls, soothing and comforting, while small hands circled Mel's neck, the little figure crushing against her, feather light lips touching her cheek.

Mel blinked, took a breath, and released the girl, speechless.

"Happy Christmas to you, Miss Parker," Mary said. "I hope you will stay. We are having games every night, and Grandmama is planning a grand party for Uncle's wedding and Twelfth Night."

"Of course, we will stay," Hermione said.

Still groping for words, Mel could do no more than nod and watch the children depart with the nursemaid.

"Mrs. Turner," Lady Loughton said, "are the bedchambers for our guests prepared?"

"Yes, I had the girls ready the beds before Christmas Eve, milady, and we've just lit the fires."

"Lady Hermione, Miss Parker, Mrs. Turner is our housekeeper. I fear she's a bit harried today as we've given much of the staff a half-day's holiday. You'll want to rest before dinner. She'll show you to your rooms, if you're ready."

"Thank you, yes." Mel stood. She would find that bedchamber and stay there until she could determine a way to escape to the Swan and continue her journey, with or without Lady Hermione Gravelston. Perhaps she could hire a maid in town and proceed north on her own. Yes, that would be best.

Hermione reached for the teapot, her lips forming a smug smile. "I'd rather like a second cup of tea, and more time to chat. If you have time, Lady Neda."

The two older ladies exchanged a long look and both sets of eyes turned to Mel.

Stomach roiling and tumbling again, she swallowed hard, taking in a breath meant to settle her insides. She knew exactly what they would be chatting about. Herself. And Fitzhenry Lovelace, Lord Loughton. And their engagement, which she had just made clear was no more.

She cast her cousin a glare and nodded, tersely. She must get herself to the coaching inn and thence to her refuge in Durham. But first, she must find a place to discreetly settle her unhappy stomach.

"Thank you, my lady," she said, and followed the housekeeper out into the corridor.

A rich carpet ran the length of the corridor, stretched between the paneled and wainscoted walls, and oil lamps hung at intervals between paintings of landscapes. It was altogether far more elegant than any home she'd ever lived in, and there had been many over the course of Papa's military career. Her natural habitat was far less refined than this, but she was more comfortable there.

Mrs. Turner bent and picked up something from the floor, *tsking* over it. She tucked the object into the deep pocket of her smock.

"Was that a ball?" Mel asked.

"I do beg your pardon, Miss. The children sometimes play bowls here."

Elegant and yet not altogether formal. That last bit made her feel less of a fish out of water.

They reached the stair landing and Mel spotted the long kissing bough hanging there.

"The girls put that up, Miss Cassandra and Miss Nancy, and their guest, Miss Cartwright. You'll meet Miss Nancy at dinner. The two older girls are away visiting some of Miss Cartwright's relations for a few days."

Mel paused to stare up at the massive clump of greenery studded with white berries. It was a fanciful item, reminding her of a Yuletide party in Colchester where three of Papa's officers had kissed her and then proposed, one after the other. On the same night. The nodcocks had all been deep in their cups, and of course, she'd refused them and refrained from telling Papa. Had he known he would've packed them off to the Peninsula that very night.

"Your room is just here." The housekeeper pointed down the continuing corridor. "Second door on the right."

The nudge was subtle, and politely done, and it jarred Mel out of her woolgathering. They were short-staffed and Mrs. Turner must be terribly busy.

"We've no maid to spare, so I'll help you out of your gown if you'd like to rest now."

Quiet footsteps behind them made them both turn. Mel's heart plummeted and rose again with a fresh wave of the nausea she thought she'd conquered.

CHAPTER THREE

Master Fitz

A gentleman had arrived on the landing, and now stood directly under the mistletoe. His blue eyes locked with hers and his smile slowly faded to shock and then something like dismay, or perhaps even horror.

Her stomach made a great leaping somersault and air whooshed from her as she remembered: resting her cheek against his bare shoulder, raking her fingers through the thick tousled hair, and the touch of his lips, so soft yet commanding...

But he wasn't happy to see her. Of course, he wasn't. No more so than she was to see him. Fitz had frozen in place under the mistletoe, paralyzed, shocked, utterly devoid of his usual charm. Or perhaps the charm had been a drawing room façade.

A bedroom façade as well.

She swallowed again. Very well, she would break the silence. "Mr. Love, er, I suppose it is Lord Loughton now." She took a step closer.

Not too close. He was, after all, standing under the mistletoe. Though she had little to worry about. She'd rendered him speechless; any closer and he might actually recoil.

Anger sparked in her. "You are surprised to see me. I am surprised to be here, as well."

"Not...not at all, I—"

"No." She shook her head. "Don't pretend you're not surprised. You didn't know either that your mother invited my cousin to visit on our way to..."

A wave of nausea swelled in her and she gulped it back. And in fact, he didn't need to know her destination. The future they'd planned had been no more than a passing whim on his part and wishful thinking on hers.

"I'm sorry to have intruded. I've informed your mother already." The tea bubbled inside her. She tasted the biscuit she'd nibbled. "I release you from any promises made. From our so-called engagement." Her cheeks flamed. Oh, Hades, she must make quick work of this. "You are free to marry... *oh.*" Hand pressed to her mouth, she hurried to the door the housekeeper had pointed to, rushing around the servant, desperately seeking a basin of some sort.

She found her way to the screened washstand and its china basin and bent over, retching, hands braced on the table.

Strong arms came around her and the air filled with the scent of horses and a man's soap.

She squeezed her eyes shut and quietly cursed a stream of whispered, unladylike oaths. As a girl who'd been raised by a soldier had a right to do. And she didn't give a fig what Fitzhenry Lovelace thought of her. Not anymore.

"I said, I release you. Go away." And once she was alone, she would cast herself on the big bed she'd spotted in the middle of this room, gown, stays, boots and all, until she was composed enough to leave for the inn.

Instead of complying, he tugged her closer. "Mrs. Turner." His breath feathered her ear, his deep voice thrumming. "Send the kitchen maid up with some dry toast and some ginger tea." A calloused finger lifted a lock of hair from her face. "No, strike that, the tea will take too long. Bring good clear drinking water, and be quick, please."

Eyes firmly shut, she waited for the housekeeper, or some other female, his mother perhaps, to come to her rescue.

Or perhaps, they wouldn't. He was the master of this house.

"Go away." She huffed out the words, another spasm unsettling her.

"You are ill."

"I don't travel well. Go away. We are finished."

"Mel." Warm lips touched the back of her neck. "Dear Mel."

A shiver went through her. One hand slipped from around her waist, and she felt a tug at her back. *Good heavens*. He meant to undress her.

"No," she said. "Mrs. Turner will—"

"She's gone off to the kitchens."

"You shouldn't *be* here." *Nor should I, blast it all*. "This is my bedchamber."

"You're very ill. And I recall that I've been in your bedchamber before."

The other arm slipped away, and cool air touched her back. Opening her eyes, she glanced into the mirror over the washstand and found him watching her.

"You're paler than you ought to be, Mel," he said, real concern on his face. "Are you certain it's not the influenza?"

His father had been struck down by the influenza, quite suddenly and dramatically. Fitz's ensuing rush to the sickbed, the death watch, the burial, the settling of the estate, the visits to solicitors and government officials, and of course the grief... Having watched her own father die, she didn't have to imagine. Fitz had been through much, and with time and distance, he'd had an opportunity to reconsider his hasty commitment to a spinster whose only attraction was the dangling possibility that her very, very, very rich grandfather might relent and leave her a fortune.

Mr. Love—Lord Loughton knew that, aside from a small bequest to her, Grandfather was holding fast to his choice to disinherit two generations of offspring. He knew because he'd heard the words himself from Grandfather's own mouth.

"Traveling sickness is not contagious." She swallowed hard against a surge of moisture.

The hand came around again holding her, this time a bit lower around her middle, and the other went back to work on her hooks. All the while, his gaze remained on her face in the mirror. He was skilled at removing a lady's gown was Fitzhenry Lovelace.

Heat chased the chill from her, memories flooding her, along with another spasm. She squeezed her eyes shut and retched again.

***

Fitz's fingers fumbled a tight hook, and while she heaved unproductively, he paused and held her. Mother's secretive smile that morning made sense now. She and Mel's cousin, Lady Hermione, had conspired to bring the two lovers together.

He was happy to have been spared the trip to Hampshire, but not at the risk of Mel's health.

She rattled with one last heave and straightened. Over the top of her head, he could see that her eyes were still tightly shut, her face in a grimace. Ill as she was, she was just herself, comfortable enough to curse like... like an infantryman. At ease with him enough to tell him to go to the devil, but never with malice. He'd loved that about her. He still did.

Hope rose in him as he set both hands to the last of the hooks, struggling to unleash them. The gown was too tight, and probably the stays as well. No wonder she was suffering.

A thought niggled at him. The gown was too tight—this was the same blue carriage gown she'd worn in September. And she was terribly nauseated.

He was the eldest of ten, and he wasn't a total idiot.

"You didn't have traveling sickness on our trip to your grandfather's."

She shrugged. "Open phaeton. Fresh air."

That was true. His sister Cassandra vomited in a closed carriage unless they kept all the windows open. And if Mel had plumped up a bit, so much the better. In fact, he'd like to have a look.

The last hook fell open and he tugged at her sleeves. "There now. Step out of the gown."

"I will when you leave," she said. "Go away."

"You're ill, Mel. We're short of servants today. It's not like you to be missish."

"How would you know?" She grumbled, but allowed the heavy gown to fall at her feet, giving him a view of her stays, and chemise, and the outline of the shapely bottom he remembered so well. She lifted one foot and then the other, while he whisked the gown away and tossed it over a chair. It was a testament to her misery that she was tolerating this.

As he started unlacing the stays, he heard the turn of the door latch and felt the cold draft that followed. China clattered.

"*Master Fitz*," Turner spluttered. "*Lord Loughton. Sir.*"

He glanced over his shoulder and saw the censure on Turner's face.

A laugh bubbled up in him, a moment of lightness. Of pure joy. Turner had known him his whole life, was fond of saying in private moments that she'd changed his clouts.

"It's not proper," Turner said. "Let me—"

"It's done." The loosened stays slipped down to Mel's hips. He pulled at the cord where it had caught and they fell all the way to the floor.

Again, Mel lifted one foot and then the other.

"A robe, Turner," Fitz said as he scattered the pins holding together her drooping coiffure.

"I've not had a chance to unpack the lady's..."

Long and lustrous, her dark and very straight hair fell to her waist. He combed his fingers through it, remembering their nights together, and how it had hung like a veil around her.

He took in a breath. *Steady, Fitz.* "Get one of my banyans."

"Your mother—"

"My bedchamber is close." He paused. Next door in fact. Mother knew that when she assigned this room to Miss Parker. He held in a chuckle and wrapped an arm around Mel. Under the thin chemise, she was all warm woman.

His woman, and soon to be his lady. He wouldn't let her go. Especially not if she was...

He truly wasn't an idiot, at least, not entirely. The Exchange often baffled him, but not these sorts of matters. What they'd started in early autumn might certainly be bearing fruit, and he wouldn't abandon her.

Plus, there was the fact that even Mel Parker's honest grumbling made his heart dance.

"I don't need a robe," she mumbled. "I just want to lie down."

"Go on then, milord," Turner said, watching him help her to the bed. "It's not proper for you to—"

"Mel is my fiancée," he said.

The lady in question spluttered and glared up at him. Turner still hovered.

He seated Mel on the bed, then crossed the room, steering the housekeeper into the corridor.

Turner's mouth firmed and she faced him, hands propped on her hips. "I just heard her break off your engagement, Master Fitz."

"She's not feeling well."

"Maybe it'd be for the best to break it off. For Miss Mary's sake. Miss Parker is nothing like Lady Alice."

Turner must have heard Mel's infantry curses. His late wife, Alice, had been a proper lady, a true English rose. She'd been dead over a year now, she and her babe who'd arrived stillborn.

"Yes." He squeezed the housekeeper's chapped hands. "Miss Parker is nothing like my late wife at all. You don't know her yet, but you'll find that *this* lady is delightful. And *this* lady, I *love*."

He closed the door on Turner's shocked face and braced a hand on the door frame. Had he said that out loud?

Certainty flooded him. He'd bollocksed up a great deal in the past few years. The marriage to

Alice had, outwardly, been perfect, a happy union of two stately families. So everyone had thought. It had taken months and months before Alice conceived Mary, and then more months of a difficult confinement. After watching nine squawking siblings arrive, one after the other, he'd never expected the wallop of sentiment that hit him the moment he held his newborn baby girl. He hadn't cared that there wasn't a baby every year to add to the nursery. He had five brothers. One of them would eventually breed an heir, it didn't have to be him.

With a moan and a gagging noise, Mel was up again. He hurried back to her.

She was too ill to suffer teasing, and far too ill for him to make love to her. Her face had grown wan, dark circles starting under her eyes.

He held her through a series of spasms, and then helped her back to bed, tucked her under the covers, and handed her a towel.

"Thank you," she mumbled.

His heart lifted. *Thank you*, not *go away*. He slid a hand under her shoulders and held a glass to her parched lips. "Take a sip, my love."

She complied without comment, a testament to how poorly she felt.

Setting the glass aside, he reached for the toast. "And the tiniest morsel of this."

She again, complied, and then fell back with a glare that made him want to stretch next to her and hold her.

Perhaps a little teasing wouldn't hurt. "Look how obedient you are."

She flopped an arm over her eyes. "I'm miserable. My head hurts. I'm peckish, and parched, and everything that goes down comes up. Go away."

That was more like his Mel. He set aside the glass and dish. "I would lie down with you, but that might push Turner into an apoplexy."

"Don't even think it," she grumbled.

Perhaps later. "You'll feel better after you rest a while, and then we'll have dinner together." He pressed his lips to her forehead. She was a trifle warm.

When he settled a damp cloth on her, she groaned. He moved an armchair to the side of the bed and sat, watching as her breathing slowed and she surrendered to sleep.

CHAPTER FOUR

A Not So Innocent Kiss

25 September 1822
Bedfordshire

"We'll stop at that inn." Fitz couldn't free up his hand to point, as busy as he was managing his pair of high-steppers. "The horses can't go on."

Nor could she, but he knew she'd never admit it. Best to appeal to her consideration for the dumb beasts. Though he'd put up the hood of his phaeton, it couldn't protect them from the downpour. The skirt of her gown was soaked, as were her half boots. Not that she'd complained.

While a groom led the horses to shelter, the innkeeper ushered Fitz and Mel into a private parlor where a fire had been lit. Miss Parker removed her wet bonnet and gloves and stretched her hands over the rising warmth.

"I've ordered tea. If you wish, I'll withdraw to the common room—"

"For the sake of my reputation?" She waved a hand. "Don't be silly. It's a dining room. There is no bed or chaise longue in sight. Tell them I'm your sister if you're concerned."

That gesture was very like the old man's that afternoon. One could believe she'd been raised by her grandfather, though she'd only just met the man. He carried two chairs over to the fire for them.

She sat and stretched her feet to the fender. "I'm not important enough to have my reputation ruined. I'm not likely to marry. I'd planned to live on the money my father left me. And if my grandfather adds to that, I'll live quite comfortably."

She'd be able do so in a small cottage in a small village, far from civilization. But how she'd manage her investments from there, he couldn't imagine.

"Mr. Sawley didn't seem entirely heartless. What could have happened that he won't leave you more? That he won't leave your mother anything?" It was none of his business, but the question had been plaguing him. Duty to family had been drilled into him and his siblings since birth by both of their parents.

She leveled a long look at him, her dark eyes filled with intelligence but no anger. "My grandfather knows your father. You truly don't know?"

He searched his memory. "Father isn't a gossip. Neither is Mother."

"Are you?"

"I can respect a confidence."

She nodded. "At fifteen my mother eloped to Scotland, and my birth came quickly enough to assume that she and my father anticipated their vows. There. I've told you everything."

"He never forgave her? What if she'd been abandoned? Or left destitute?"

She turned back to the fire, her mouth firming. He'd finally gone too far. Or...there was more she didn't wish to share with him.

"My *father* was an officer in the King's Army and an honorable man. He always provided for us, and when he died, he wisely tied up her dower to provide her with a steady income. No one in their right mind would hand my mother a pile of money."

The former Mrs. Parker must be like his late friend Glanford, who'd diligently spent every penny that came his way and then some.

She sighed. "In truth, her new husband is not penniless. Though I imagine part of the reason they went to Bordeaux was to stretch their shillings."

Or dodge creditors. That was often the case. "It's a wonder they didn't take you with them."

A shiver went through her. "I'd spent much time with Lady Hermione and her late husband through the years when Papa was away. They were childless, you know, and always welcoming. As soon as Papa was buried and the will settled, I happily let Hermione gather me up and take me home to her cottage in Hampshire."

A maid entered carrying a tray.

"Oh, good." Miss Parker stood. "Come along, Brother, and I'll pour."

She busied herself, silently serving until the door closed. "Your parents aren't gossips, Mr. Lovelace, but I'll ask you again, are *you*?"

She leveled another long look, one that hinted of a vulnerability that touched his heart.

"You saved me today, Miss Parker." Let her believe that. In truth, he'd been plotting for days, seeking a way to spend more time with her. "I owe you my silence, and yes, I'll tell you again, I'm capable of keeping private matters private. You have my word as a gentleman."

She studied him a long moment, color rising in her cheeks, before reaching her hand across the table and grinning. "We must shake on it."

Her face lit with an intelligence, and playfulness, and open-hearted good nature that stirred him. A man might be comfortable with a woman like Miss Parker.

He took the hand offered, flipped it over, and pressed his lips to her palm in a kiss that set her whole face aflame and his own heart beating wildly.

CHAPTER FIVE

Resolved to End Things

28, December 1822
Loughton Manor, Leicestershire

Mel opened her eyes to a garden of blue and pink flowers, curling and bursting on the underside of the bed canopy.

Her neck ached, and when she turned her pounding head to the side, it felt like a rattling dried gourd. Across the room, a stream of bright light sliced through a gap in the window curtains.

She sat up and looked around. The bed was large, the chamber well furnished with a sofa and chairs, and this elegant tester bed with its crisp white sheets. A carved wooden mantel framed a hearth and the bright fire casting warmth into the room. An armchair had been drawn up to the bedside.

She fell back, remembering. Hermione had tricked her. They were at Loughton Manor, and though she'd informed Fitz that he was a free man, he'd held her, undressed her, put her to bed, and then hovered in that very chair.

For how long? She pressed her hands to her face. What time was it? Had it been only an hour or two since she'd fallen asleep, or was that morning light? They'd arrived here in a gloomy midafternoon that threatened more snow, but perhaps the skies had cleared and the sun was setting, and...

Dinner. *We'll have dinner together.*

He'd murmured the words in her ear, and then she'd felt the touch of his lips.

Warmth uncurled in her, and this time it wasn't her stomach rebelling. She pushed down the sudden desire, just as she'd fought the nausea for the last few days. The last several days.

Oh, very well, the last many weeks.

It wasn't what Hermione suspected, dropping broad hints about Fitzhenry Lovelace, their scandalous afternoon at the inn, and her courses. Surely it couldn't be that. Mother had managed only once to... No. She and Hermione had returned to Hampshire and some spoiled cheese. Or perhaps it had been the oysters they'd eaten at the inn on the way home that started everything. In any case, Hermione had recovered, but Mel's own more sensitive stomach had not.

A distant thump reminded her that there'd been other noises the night before: voices at her bedside, Hermione's, and another lady's gentle tones. The pixie, Fitz's mother, most likely. There'd been knocks on the door, footsteps across the room, whispers, and now that she thought about it, even some shouting and giggling and running feet in the corridor.

She rubbed her eyes and sat up, pressing a hand to her stomach. Hunger gnawed at her insides, blessedly unaccompanied by nausea. She must find something to eat.

Swinging her legs over the side of the bed, she spotted a glass of water on the bedside table and took a deep swallow. The pain between her eyebrows eased.

A teapot sat on the table near the fire. She tossed aside the covers and reached for her robe—which someone had unpacked from her trunk and placed at the foot of the bed.

He was pampering her, or his mother was. Or perhaps they were this kind to all their guests, especially those who were ill. Though she doubted Fitz served anyone else as lady's maid, at least not in his mother's home.

Remembering the housekeeper's shock made her chuckle.

Nevertheless, she must be firm with Fitz—and with herself. Fitz's abandonment and her mother's expected arrival had forced her to make a new plan, and she would see it through. His solicitousness wouldn't change her mind, and she would tell him that when next they spoke.

She must end things with him and be on her way. Mother had left the reading of Papa's will in a huff and a flurry, torn between badgering Mel for money and rushing the slippery Lord Starling to the altar. It was entirely possible that Mother didn't know about the cottage in Durham. With luck, when she found Mel missing from Hampshire, she would retreat to her husband's manor in Kent until spring.

The tea had gone cold, but Mel poured a cup anyway, and helped herself to a cake from the tray. When everything stayed down, and her stomach didn't rebel, she set herself to searching for her things. No clothes press graced this room, but there'd been a washstand behind a screen and a dressing table.

The scene at the washstand had been a humiliating moment, but never mind. Surely no man wanted to see a lady engaged in tossing up all of her insides. If it put him off her, so much the better.

Someone had carefully placed her comb and brush. She gazed into the small mirror, remembering his face looking back at her with kindness and concern. He had been altogether unbearably handsome. And, considering his neglect, false. Certainly that.

An ornamental dish held her pins. He'd taken her hair down, scattering pins, as was his wont. Someone had kindly gathered them from the carpet.

Despite the wisps of remembered voices and noises, she'd slept through all of the unpacking and tidying-up. Papa always said she slumbered far too soundly to make a good soldier. An enemy could take her unawares.

She shrugged off the ghost of Fitz's face in the mirror and put a hand to her hair. Straight as a stick it might be, but it was the devil to untangle when it was like this. With a sigh, she picked up the comb and crossed the room to the chair by the fire and began combing out knots.

CHAPTER SIX

The Proposal

25 September 1822
Lady Clitheroe's Estate, Bedfordshire

The quiet tapping started soon after Hermione departed Mel's bedchamber.

What now?

Her cousin had not quite wrung a peel over Mel's head, but she had been displeased. Not so much about Mel's and Mr. Lovelace's late return to Lady Clitheroe's, both of them bedraggled and wet after being *alone together* most of the day. Their dramatic arrival had stirred concern from their hostess, winks from the male guests, and glares from the young ladies stalking Mr. Lovelace.

Mel was, in a word, ruined. What nonsense. She pulled out a pin from her tangled coiffure.

Though Mr. Lovelace was appealing, a forced marriage to him—Hermione's first impulse—reminded her of the one her mother had been planning for her. The thought of coercing an unwilling party to marry was abhorrent.

When she dismissed the suggestion, Hermione's true concern became clear. Ruination required an early departure from Lady Clitheroe's excellent cook and a swift return to the genteel poverty of Hermione's Hampshire cottage.

The secret visit to Grandfather had also displeased her. For that, Mel felt a trifle guilty. But only a trifle, because Hermione would have wheedled the man for money, and Mel's pride couldn't have borne that. She'd sent Hermione off and prepared to deal with her own hair.

The tapping grew louder, probably the maid Hermione had sent away. She would do the same. Combing out her own tangles would give her much needed time to think.

She rose from the seat by the fire clutching her comb.

The latch rattled, the door eased open, and a figure entered.

She gasped. "Mr. Lovelace."

He quietly closed the door and took her hands. "You are well?" he asked.

He'd changed to dry clothing and was fully dressed, while she was in her nightgown and robe.

"Yes," she said, distracted by the warmth radiating from him, remembering his kiss on her *palm*, for heaven's sake. "What are you doing here?"

"Your cousin did not berate you too badly?"

She scoffed and smiled. "She'll greatly miss the fine meals when we return home. We'll leave the day after tomorrow."

He pried the comb from her hand and drew her closer to the fire, seating her and then kneeling before her.

Alarm bells clanged, a cannon boomed along with them, and every one of her nerves tingled as they had in the inn when he'd pressed his lips to that most sensitive part of her hand. She'd been wooed by men just as handsome; men both strong- and weak-willed, men who were crafty and men who were dolts. The army had men of every variety, and though she'd come close, she'd never lost her head. Or her maidenhead.

Yet.

"We must talk," he said.

She inwardly shook herself. "If you recall, talking is what caused our delay." They'd talked on the journey to Grandfather's, and again after they'd left. And then, his innocent-but-not-innocent kiss had loosened her tongue even further—and his. They'd talked through the late afternoon and into the evening, through a meal and another round of tea. They'd shared stories about their childhoods and he'd spoken with such a deep fondness of his parents, and siblings, and nieces, and daughter that she'd been more than a little touched.

They'd also talked of investments and politics and trade. The rain had lifted long before they'd departed the inn.

"Yes, and I don't regret one moment of it," he said. "Will you make me the happiest of men? Will you marry me, Miss Parker?"

"*Marry*?" The cannon in her chest boomed again. "Don't be s-silly."

He seated himself next to her and kissed her, a soft press of his lips to hers, sweetness laced with a heated promise of more.

She drew away. "It's not necessary. You don't need to save me."

"I see that I need to convince you. How shall I go about it?" He traced his fingers over her cheek and onward. A pin flew, and a lock of hair slipped over her shoulder. "You being you, I'll start with the pragmatic reasons." His breath tickled her ear as he leaned close, spotting and removing hairpins. "Even as we speak, there are gossips in their bedchambers writing letters to friends reporting on our absence together, alone, for the whole day; our stop at an inn together, alone, and our return."

Together. Alone.

More pins and hair fell, like the elements of her plan scattering about her.

"Your grandfather's recommendation that you marry the proper sort of man is a sound one. You are knowledgeable, Miss Parker. Brilliant, actually. Courageous, but not foolish. I could tell that from your conversation with Mr. Sawley. And I have a seat in the Commons."

It went without saying that he would have a seat in the Lords when his father died, but he'd made it very clear to her that afternoon that he loved his father as much as she'd loved hers, and was in no hurry to claim the title.

The remains of her coiffure collapsed, and his fingers combed through her hair.

"You're brilliant, and you're beautiful, Miss Parker. Mary Elizabeth."

"Mel," she whispered.

"Mel?"

"It's what my close family call me."

"Mine call me Fitz for Fitzhenry."

The name suited him, noble as well as seductively derived from the French. "Son of Henry?"

"Yes. Henry is my father's name."

He said no more, only watched her, steady and unblinking, while her heart thumped and clanged and she tumbled into his midnight blue gaze. His full lips quirked, his hands reached for her and she went willingly.

Master Fitz's Fatal Failing

28 December 1822
Loughton Manor, Leicestershire

The door latch turned, setting Mel's nerves on edge, but it was only Hermione.

"You're awake." Hermione opened the door wider for the sturdy young maid behind her who carried a pitcher and towels. "This is Maggie, come to dress you and do your hair, and then you and I will go down to breakfast."

"Breakfast? I slept the afternoon and night through?"

"You did. And Lord Loughton by your side well into the evening. It took Lady Neda herself to pull him away to join the children at dinner, and then later, to send him off to his own bed. He was so worried about you he would have sent for the midwife—"

"*The midwife?*"

Hermione waved a hand. "She being the only medical practitioner available. Their surgeon has gone off to visit his family for the Yuletide, and the apothecary has come down with a lung fever. Isn't that right, Maggie?"

"Yes, madam. Mrs. Astrop's been ever so busy. Run ragged, she says, what with babies picking their arrivals in the worst weather and folks needing medicine for the lung fever."

The maid had just returned through a side door with a fresh chemise, stockings, and her stays.

"I'll go and pick out a dress." Hermione swished over to the same side door. "Your best gown, I think."

"My carriage gown will do."

"No, it will not. You're not running off anywhere today. Not as ill as you were yesterday."

We'll see about that. Mel stood and submitted to being dressed. "Who is here? Surely all of the Lovelace family are not present." Dear God, she hoped not.

"No, not at all, miss," Maggie said. "Mr. George left yesterday with Lady Glanford, and Mr. Selwyn and Mr. Rupert stayed in London for the Yuletide. Mr. Fitz's married sisters are away also, spending the season with their families. And his sister, Miss Cassandra has gone off for a week with her friend, Miss Cartwright."

In September, Fitz had provided a list of his family members, but trying to remember all of them made her dizzy. "So who is left?"

"Well, there's her ladyship, his mother, and himself, of course, and his sister Miss Nancy, and the boys, Master James and Master Edward, and Lady Glanford's little Lord Glanford and Master Ben, and his lordship's Miss Mary."

"Mostly children." How astonishing.

"You like children." Hermione had returned carrying the one good day dress Mel donned for village social events. "It will be very jolly."

"It's a wonder Lord Loughton didn't stay at that hunting party."

"He planned to," Maggie said, "and right riled up he was when her ladyship sent Mr. George to fetch him back."

Mel shared a long look with Hermione. In a great house like this, there was no better source of information than a gossipy servant. Hermione, she knew, would not mind her probing. How else was one to learn anything?

"I suppose Lady Loughton wanted him here when I arrived," Mel said.

"Oh, that wasn't why. It had to do with young Lord Glanford and little Master Ben." Maggie cheerfully cinched and tied the stays then reached for the gown. "Why, this blue will set off the shine in your hair, if I do say so myself."

"I recall that Lord Glanford was a particular friend of Lord Loughton," Hermione mused. "No doubt Lady Neda wanted him to spend time with the boys."

"'Tweren't that, not entirely. He's the boys' guardian and hadn't been tending to them."

Mel glanced back at the girl who was fastening her gown. "What do you mean?"

Maggie's hands paused and her cheeks colored. "Beg pardon, miss. I've spoken out of turn. His lordship is ever such a good man, but with all that happened, his wife and the babe dying and the old lord's sudden passing... sure and he didn't mean to neglect his wards for so long, and he must be ever so sorry... and with Mr. George taking him to task and then taking Lady Glanford to wife, all will be well." She took in a breath, her color still high. "If you'll sit now, I'll do up your hair, which, if I do say so, is ever so shiny and lovely. And if you've time I can tease a few curls—"

"No, do not bother with curls. A simple twist and a tuck will do."

While Maggie bit her tongue and worked, Mel fumed and counted her blessings.

On the evidence of several days and two eventful nights, she'd pledged herself to an honorable man. Or so she'd thought.

Oh, Hades, she'd been dazzled by his handsome face, and his kisses, and the way he'd made her feel. The way he still made her feel. And Grandfather had given his blessings to their betrothal.

And then—*out of sight, out of mind*—his letters had tapered off and stopped. He'd swiftly fallen out of the love he'd declared. Having lived among soldiers and seen the male species at close view, she shouldn't be surprised.

But neglecting those boys...

Maggie tucked in the last pin and stood back.

"Well done," Hermione said.

Mel studied her reflection. A few curls tickled her cheeks and altogether softened her appearance. "How did you manage it? It usually takes me half the day to produce a curl. Thank you."

Pleased, Maggie smiled and began tidying the room, but Mel sent her away and turned on her cousin. "Did you know of this business about Fitz and Glanford's boys?'

Hermione chewed on her lip and sighed. "Neda hinted at trouble."

"He *neglected* them."

"There is always another side to every story."

"Two innocent boys in his charge? What other side could there be that would be honorable?" Mel scrubbed her knuckles over her cheeks. "I just want to leave. What if Mother has arrived in

Hampshire and decided to find us? What if she appears here at Loughton Manor?"

"She won't trouble herself to make that long of a journey."

"She might, if as you say, she's taken a notion that Grandfather will leave me money. She might learn that he's been ill. She always had ways of finding things out. She might know of the cottage in Durham after all." Heaven help her if Mother appeared there. Where could she go then?

Father's old batman lived near the cottage. Perhaps he would take pity on her and offer sanctuary. "No, you go down and I'll go out through the kitchen and take a gig to the inn and proceed on. I'll leave half my purse—"

"*Mary Elizabeth*. Running is not the answer. And it's not like you to be a coward."

"I'm not..." She took in a deep breath. She'd been cowardly aplenty lately, and running away was in her blood, from the womb, one might say. Mother had run off more than once, always with a lover. Papa had run from time to time, as well, though he'd passed it off as answering the call of duty, leaving Mel to cope with Mother, or to take refuge with Hermione.

She must be stronger than them. She *was* stronger, drat it. She'd made one mistake, she who'd deflected bounders and rascals all her life. "You're right. I must settle this once and for all. I shall be brave. I shall go down to breakfast."

"And be cordial with the family."

She thought of Mary's soft kiss on her cheek. But surely, Mary would breakfast in the nursery, and it would only be Fitz and his mother to be dealt with. "Of course."

"And you must give him a chance to explain."

Explain turning his back on his wards? His friends' two minor sons?

He might *try* to explain the unconscionable. After breakfast, if he wished to do so, she would listen, and then she would leave.

Good cheer warmed the breakfast room, as brightly as the morning sun streaming in the windows. Pine boughs and ribbons draped the mantel, and sprigs of holly with bright red berries filled a bowl on the table. Curious faces beamed at her as she entered, a smiling Mary getting up on her knees in the chair next to the pixie, who called out a greeting to both her and her cousin.

"*Mel.*" Fitz rose from his seat at the head of the table, a look of relief blooming into a welcoming smile that heated her down to her toes.

The gray-eyed boy she'd met yesterday sat at his left, an older version of the boy at Fitz's right. The rest of the group, two older school-age boys and a girl probably old enough for her come-out, all blond-haired like Fitz, examined her closely, their blue eyes curious but not unfriendly.

Fitz hurried around the table to her, taking her hands and gazing down at her. "Are you feeling better?" His neckcloth was perfectly tied, his coat brushed, his collar starched to sharp points, but his hair was deliciously tousled, and the warmth in his eyes...

A lump lodged in her throat. She swallowed it down, nodding, and reminded herself to resist his charms.

Introductions were made, and he seated her at the foot of the table and fetched her a plate. The aroma of egg and bacon sent her stomach into a flutter, and she reached for the corner of toast.

Returning to his seat, Fitz gave the older gray-eyed boy, Lord Glanford, a fond tap on the head, and the boy glowed up at him.

What had Maggie said? He must be ever so sorry. Perhaps, where the boys were concerned, Fitz had patched things up. But it had taken his own mother's strong will and his brother's strong arm to do so. What honorable man required such intervention to do what was right?

"Are you coming with us today, Miss Parker?" Fitz's sister, Nancy, asked. "We're attending a party—a *children's* party. I would very much like to not be the only young lady there, alone with all these nodcocks."

"Oh. I..." A party? No wonder Mary's red frock was trimmed in green, and more festive green and red ribbons adorned the bodice of Nancy's white gown.

Nancy smiled, and she couldn't help think that the frank, jolly girl might have the makings of a friend, if she were to stay. Which she wouldn't.

Nancy's brother, James, smirked, and the younger of the two Lovelace boys, Edward laughed.

Lady Loughton set her teacup aside. "You won't be the only young lady, Nancy. Your friends will be there. Though if you are well enough, Miss Parker, we would love to have you come and meet all our neighbors. You as well, Lady Hermione."

"I believe I will go," Hermione said with an overbright smile that meant she was angling to leave Fitz and Mel alone. "Nothing better than a Yuletide fête, especially one for children. So much vitality there."

"And tonight, Grandmama has promised a scavenger hunt." Mary was still on her knees, and no one in this lively group had corrected her. "But will you come with us this morning, Miss Parker? There will be games, and cakes, and even a puppet show."

A smile tugged at Mel's lips, and she gave into it. "I fear I'd best not, sweet one. Though it does sound very jolly."

"But what will you do here, all by yourself?" That had come from Edward.

"She'll spend the day with me," Fitz said.

"You're not going, Fitz?"

James's exclamation opened a flurry of loud conversation among the siblings, even some yelling. Good heavens, they were not just lively— they were wild.

No wonder Fitz wanted to stay home. He was avoiding a raucous children's party—look how he'd treated his wards.

She swallowed again, fighting her mouthful of egg to stay down. "I *should* like to speak with you, Lord Loughton, but I won't take up much of your time. You would still be able to go."

His gaze fixed on her, melting her resolve.

"With last night's snowfall, we'll need to leave immediately to allow for the roads." Fitz's mother stood, and all the boys jumped up, including her eldest. "Come along then, children. Lady Hermione, join us in the hall after you have finished your breakfast."

Mary clambered off the chair and threw herself into Fitz's arms for a farewell hug.

Hermione's cup clanged against the saucer. "I'm quite ready now." While the children hurried out, Hermione paused by Mel's chair and whispered, "You two lovebirds use this time wisely."

"We are not..." *Oh never mind.* Skirts rustled as her cousin and Lady Loughton departed.

Fitz appeared next to her, his subtle cologne filling her senses. She fidgeted with her napkin.

"You've not eaten much of your eggs. Are you still feeling ill?"

"I'm fine."

His thumb swept her cheek. His other fingers eased her chin his way and the sight of him sent her heart into a desperate pounding. Strong nose and jaw and oh so kissable lips, and the tiniest of clefts in his chin. His deep-set blue eyes were filled with a sadness that resonated within her.

She inwardly shook herself. That was merely her being fanciful, as fanciful as her histrionic mother.

CHAPTER EIGHT

A Confession

As the breakfast room emptied of children and servants, Fitz contemplated Mel. How beautiful she was, with her gleaming dark eyes and hair, her proud chin and lush mouth. Her father had claimed Spanish nobility somewhere in his bloodline. Her mother's side was thoroughly English. Though Mel had said little about her mother, she'd been close to her father, a proud soldier, a steady and honorable man who, in one impetuous moment of passion, had eloped with a banker's flighty daughter.

Mel was spirited but not flighty. At Lady Clitheroe's he'd noticed her holding back, her eyes lit with amusement as other young ladies hounded him. Over several days, he'd watched her tease the wallflowers out of their nerves and engage the younger men in cards and games, always with the playfulness of an older sibling. Besides being beautiful, she was comfortable and kind.

A sense of what he had to lose swept through him. Too absorbed in his own troubles, he'd taken her promise to marry him for granted. He'd taken *her* for granted. He'd hurt her.

Had he done that to Alice?

He shook off the thought. With Alice, there'd been fault on both sides.

"Lord Loughton, you ought to go to that party with your family and your wards."

She lifted his fingers away from her cheek, but he held on to her hand. "The parish children's party is always a merry time, but I wouldn't miss the chance to talk things over with you."

"What is there to say? You are set free. I will leave."

"And go where?"

"That is not your concern."

"You and Hermione setting out on the road in this weather, just the two of you?" It most certainly was his concern. "I would worry. And go where, Mel?"

She squeezed her eyes tight and her lips trembled. The threat of tears gave him hope.

"Oh, very well. Papa left me a cottage and a small holding."

"Where?"

"In the north."

"North of here? The roads are dreadful in Yorkshire, my brother George said." And she'd set out on this journey in the middle of winter instead of sensibly waiting until spring. *Why?*

There must be a good reason. Mother had hinted that Lady Hermione was pockets to let. Mel's small income from her father's bequest would suffice if she owned the cottage outright, if it wasn't falling down about her and in need of expensive repairs. Her grandfather had promised to leave a small bequest. Though he'd been ill recently, Sawley, as far as he knew, was still alive.

"Nevertheless, I will journey on," she said. "I'm not afraid of the weather."

Their intertwined hands drew her attention, and she chewed on her lip, blinking prodigiously. A tear slid down her cheek.

"Oh, Mel."

With a quiet curse, she straightened her shoulders. "I don't know why I'm such a watering-pot lately. You have always been too kind to me. When we're together, that is. Let us leave it at that and go our separate ways." She shivered and turned to the fire.

Stubborn woman. He wouldn't give up so easily. Or at all. "Come with me to the study and let me tell you about the weeks since we've been apart. There's a good fire there. I can even show you the estate books and you might have some advice for me."

Her lips firmed, making him want to soften them with his own. When she stood and took the arm he offered, hope stirred in him. He'd win her back. He'd change her mind about leaving. He could ride to the bishop for a license and be married before his brother George tied the knot with Sophie. Or... Mother had reminded him that the banns had already been called. There was no need whatsoever to wait.

He led her up the stairs to the cozy room where just three nights earlier, Mother, George, and Sophie had laid all his incompetence out in the open.

***

The room he led her to had a few shelves, a cabinet, and chairs, but a massive mahogany desk held center stage, laden with correspondence, ledgers, and files. It was altogether too fusty and old fashioned for Fitz, who seemed most at home on his horse or in the seat of his phaeton, and she could never picture him immersing himself in so much paper.

He bypassed the desk and showed her to an upholstered chair near the hearth, then set to work feeding the fire, reminding her of the rainy afternoon they'd spent together in the private parlor of the Flitwick inn where they'd taken refuge.

"Are you warm enough, my dear?"

"Quite." She cleared her throat, finding a lump and trying to swallow it. "I've said my piece. If you have something to say, please proceed, so I may go on my way."

He pulled his matching chair closer. His hand, so strong and warm, came around hers, and a new wave of blubbering threatened. She must, must, *must* get hold of herself. Fitz did not love her. Why he was being so kind, she couldn't imagine.

"I spent Christmas Day reading and rereading your letters. I had planned to leave this morning and journey to Hampshire to see you. I've behaved abominably, and I wanted to explain. To beg your forgiveness for my absence and lack of attention. It's true, Father's death left me busy settling the estate and arranging matters with the title. It's also true I didn't receive all your letters right away. But..." His jaw firmed. "Here is another truth, Mel: I've made a hash of estate matters these last few months, even before Father's death. I'm not quite the wealthy man whose hand you accepted in September."

She'd accepted more than his hand. "You are telling me this...this disappearance was about money?"

Her breath left her as the realization hit: he needed a wealthy heiress.

"Yes," he said, pausing a moment too long.

Heat flared in her and then drained, and a shiver went through her. He'd used her and tossed her aside, just as Papa warned men would do. On his deathbed, her father had cautioned her that even her small income might draw a bounder. Without him to protect her, he'd urged her to be sensible.

Heavens, she was a hundred times more sensible than Mother and her husband, and perhaps even more so than her dear father.

Her vision clouded. Except with Fitz. She'd thrown herself headlong into this rash betrothal. She ought to have known her dowry wouldn't, in the long run, be enough.

"I'd heard..." She cleared her throat. "You were off to one house party or fête, or fox hunt after another." She swallowed hard, fighting a wave of emotion. What a ninny she was. "You were looking to trade up to an heiress."

"No." His hand crushed her own. "Never. I did not play you false, Mel. I would never do that."

He let go of her hand and stood, bracing himself on the mantel, staring into the fire. "Do you not recall what your grandfather told you? You need to move about in society to learn of financial opportunities. That was my purpose. Meeting friends who could help me through a rough patch."

She swallowed a scoff. What nerve he had. Her interview with Gregory Sawley had been *her* mission, *her* visit, and *her* lesson. Fitz had already learned those lessons. He'd merely tagged along with her that day.

"Did your father never need to absent himself to tend to business?"

"Of course. He was a soldier."

"Do you not remember that I said my father offered the same advice? That's why two of my brothers are in London most of the year, keeping track of investments and business opportunities."

"And they can't sell off shares or produce ready cash to help you?"

He swiped a hand through his hair. "It's not strictly money that's needed. There are some new agricultural practices to explore and... this is mine to manage. But, yes. My brothers would help, but I'd only ask it for the sake of Mother or the children. And I don't want to ask."

"You have your pride." She understood pride. Her own had been suffering immensely these last few weeks.

He fell to his knees and took her free hand. "Can you endure some small economies while I resolve this? We'll write a proper settlement agreement, as your grandfather demanded. You'll retain your inheritance and control over it. I don't want to lose your wise counsel, Mel. I don't want to lose *you*."

The pain in his face showed what it cost him in pride. Could she trust him? He hadn't said anything about love. But love could grow, couldn't it, if there was respect and understanding?

Perhaps that was the better way. She'd watched her parents thrash about, hurting each other. The passion that launched them into marriage had torched any respect or understanding they'd shared at the beginning. Perhaps Fitz's mother and father had provided him a better example of married life.

She cradled his face with her hand and swept her thumb over his freshly shaved jaw, the warmth in his eyes pulling her toward him until she was in his arms and their lips touched with a sweetness that brought tears to her eyes.

Desire flooded her in a sudden mad rush, driving out all thought except for the need to feel him. Her hands came around him, her fingers tangled into his hair even as her tongue met his. Then, lips still locked, she was floating up and then down, onto his lap.

She yanked at his neckcloth, while his hands moved over her arms, her breasts, her hips; down her skirts, and up again, his warm hands sliding over her stockings and garters and—

"Wait." Fitz pressed his forehead to hers. "Let me lock the door."

"Oh." Mel's eyes shot open. His neckcloth flapped open against the unbuttoned waistcoat and... her cheeks flamed. She'd unbuttoned his fall. "No."

She jumped off of him, pacing, pressing her hands to her cheeks. "I'm sorry." She was not just a ridiculous watering pot lately; where Fitz was concerned, she was a wanton.

Strong arms came around her. "I'm not sorry. Marry me, Mel."

No. There was a reason she couldn't. What was it?

She opened her eyes and her gaze fell on the piles of paper and files. Fitz said he wanted her counsel.

"What happened to put you in such dire financial straits?" If a man trained up to be a peer of the realm could bungle finances... there would be a lesson there for someone like herself.

His arms tensed. "Bad crops. Bad storms. A bad post-war economy. And I loaned a great deal of money to a friend."

She turned in his arms and studied him. His mouth had hardened, and he looked away.

"To whom? Why?"

"I'd recommended an investment that went bad. I'd withdrawn before it was too late, and neglected to tell him that. He'd thrown in everything and lost it, and I felt responsible. But, I've worked out a repayment agreement with Lady Glanford—"

"*Glanford?*"

"I loaned her late husband a great deal of money."

The voice was that of an angry stranger. This Fitz she didn't recognize, but she felt sure he wasn't angry with her. The anger, the loathing was aimed at Glanford.

What had Maggie said? That he'd neglected his wards. Had the anger against the father been visited upon the sons?

No, that wasn't right. She'd seen with her own eyes at breakfast that he and the boys were on good terms. There was more to this and she must prod him to tell her. How best should she go about it?

CHAPTER NINE

Confession Interrupted

Mel's gaze had narrowed on him, as direct and assessing as that of her grandfather when he and Fitz had spoken in private.

"It was damnably foolish of me. I knew it when I did it, but I felt... responsible, in a way, that he'd squandered everything."

"Everything?"

"Sophie—Lady Glanford—brought a fortune into the marriage. And yes, everything."

"I see." Her lips firmed. "You beggared your family's estate to help a scapegrace friend. You were being honorable... for the sake of his wife? His children? But why then... Lord Loughton, I was told that you neglected his sons. Your wards. Or... was that information false? Was that simply a vile rumor?"

A trickle of perspiration slid down his back. In the twelve months since Glanford's and Alice's deaths, he'd not visited his wards once or followed up on the arrangements a guardian ought to make. He'd given only a cursory attention to the business correspondence with Glanford's steward and solicitor. Since his return home Christmas Eve, he'd been over this with Mother, and George, and Sophie. Confronting his neglect hadn't eased his shame or the pain that went with it.

"It's true." He could see in Mel's eyes it was another strike against him. "I saw the boys after Glanford's funeral. I'd planned to stay long enough to see to matters there, but then news came that my late wife had gone into labor."

Three months early, or so he'd thought. The shock, the anger, the grief had been paralyzing, and all of it renewed after Father's death and the confirmation of his worst suspicions.

Mother had been right to send George for him and to invite Mel.

"With all that has happened, I've been negligent, Mel. It's true. But I assure you, I'm on good terms with the lads, and will continue to be so." Thank heavens, the boys were resilient. "Sophie is as intelligent and sensible as you. We've agreed she'll see to the management of the estate and the boys' education, and consult with me if needed. And my equally sensible brother George will soon be their stepfather. Artie and Ben will be well cared for."

"I see. You've turned your responsibilities over to their mother and your brother." She folded her arms at her waist. "I suppose that's wise." Head tilted, her scrutiny was relentless. "What more aren't you telling me?"

Her dark eyes gleamed with perceptiveness and determination. He loved that she was direct, not missish or coy. But this matter...

Outside the clouds shifted, darkening the room, and a shiver traced its way through his spine. He turned away, remembering the child he'd hoped for with such joy, the child whose conception he thought meant his marriage was finally as it should be, the dead babe he'd cradled in his arms, a big bruiser of a lad. *Not premature at all*, Mrs. Astrop, the midwife had whispered to him. Alice had thrashed about, mumbling what sounded like *sorry* before slipping into oblivion.

He'd been in London, and she in the country when that child was conceived. A dead friend, a dead wife, and a dead child—who wasn't his. It was after Father's funeral that a chance remark by an acquaintance in his cups confirmed which friend had betrayed him.

A knock at the door saved him from answering. He wrestled his fall and waistcoat into place and went to the door.

"I beg your pardon." Biggs averted his gaze from the untied neckcloth. "One of the Cruikwork lads is below asking for you."

The Cruikworks had been long-time tenants. The older son had gone off to war and returned with two stepchildren and a troublesome bride whose temper ran as hot as his own to join his parents and youngest siblings in the cottage they all shared. The arrival of more babies, the death of his father, the post-war depression, and the scars of battle he carried increased his burdens. As did Fitz's incompetence. The family's holding needed upkeep from the landlord, upkeep that he'd had to defer.

A head poked through the door. "You must hurry, me mam says, else they'll kill each other."

"I'll be right along." He turned back to Mel. "I have to go."

She glanced at young Harry Cruikwork and then back at Fitz. "Is he beating his wife?"

"Unless she's taking a turn at thrashing him," Fitz said.

She reached for his elbow and nudged him to the door. "I've been with my father when he intervened in soldiers' domestic disputes. I'm going with you."

Alice would never engage with the tenants, except as the lady of the manor bringing a food basket. Nor would he have encouraged her to do so.

But Mel was different. She was ever straightforward with him, and he wanted to be so with her as well, at least as much as he could be. It was risky, but let her see what the burdens of Loughton were like. "Fetch your boots and meet me at the stables."

Perhaps while he tackled the husband, her good sense could tame the beast in Jilly Cruikwork. Because the last thing he wanted to do was turn the man and his family out.

Mel rode along next to Fitz, the horses picking their way through snow and in some places muddy slush. She hadn't had time to change into a riding habit, but the generous cloak Fitz had flung over her covered her well, shielding her from the cold wind as she listened to his tale of the troubled family.

"Are you the Justice of the Peace?" she asked.

"Father was. I haven't taken up the mantle yet."

"What do you mean to do with..."

"Cruikwork"

"Cruikwork. Yes. Will you put him out?"

"No," he said. "Cruikwork served for years in the Peninsular campaign."

His firm answer unaccountably cheered her—unaccountably because it was probably a terrible business decision if the tenant was wreaking havoc.

On the other hand, Father had tolerated much from his men, as long as they performed on the field of battle. He'd used the lash as needed, of course.

She wondered if Fitz had a lash? Probably not. And locking the man up for a few days might only increase the family's hardship.

But the wife might be the one causing trouble. Women often did, of course. Not aristocrats or gentry perhaps, but she'd seen women in the camps tumbling about engaged in fisticuffs, usually fighting over a man, Papa had said, though it was likely more about what the man in question could provide in the way of food or security.

It put her in mind of Lady Susan and Miss Pritney at Lady Clitheroe's house party. Both of them had set their caps for Fitz. Fortunately, his friends had sniffed out their plans. On the ride to Grandfather's, she and Fitz had laughed over Lady Susan's planned snare involving meeting at the folly, and Miss Pritney's plot to push Fitz into the stream, jump in behind him, and then rip open the drop-front on her gown. Mel had advised him to tell them both to go to the devil, but his gentlemanly senses wouldn't allow it. How ironic that Mel had saved him from them, and trapped him for herself. Unintentionally, of course.

She glanced his way and saw that he was gazing ahead with a pensive stare. He was concerned about these tenants, but that wasn't all. They hadn't finished their conversation. She must ask him again about that Glanford business. Something about it was troubling him.

A screech pierced the quiet of the snow-laden elms, and Fitz kicked his horse into a faster pace. A cottage came into view, the roof draped here and there with ragged oil cloth, the chimney bricks missing mortar in various places. Out-buildings sagged around items blanketed in melting snow—debris or farm equipment, she couldn't be sure.

Dismounting quickly, they approached the open cottage door—another scarred, sagging item.

"Be done with you, you she-wolf," a man bellowed.

Fitz shoved Mel behind him, blocking her view.

She was peering around him when he suddenly ducked, taking her down with him. Crockery sailed out through the open door, making a soft landing in the muddy snow.

"Well done, Fitz," Mel said, choking back a laugh.

"You will stop this instant, Mrs. Cruikwork," Fitz said in a drawl, the lazy tone cloaking an iron will.

Gaping mouths greeted them, and Mel saw immediately one of the problems. There were entirely too many people crammed into the small cottage, all but three of them children.

"You see, Jilly." The lone man in the group puffed up his chest and preened.

"Cruikwork," Fitz said sternly, "Why is your wife sporting a swollen eye and a bloody lip?"

Mel moved up beside Fitz and surveyed the room more closely. Pots, buckets and pans stood in strategic locations collecting leaks; broken dishes and tipped over chairs littered the room, and—she did a quick count—eight children of various ages plus an older woman with a babe in each arm hovered in the corners. The tall lad who'd come to fetch Fitz wasn't here. He would make number eleven.

Good heavens. They were like the Lovelace family, a hardy lot whose children had survived.

The woman, Jilly, wore a clean but threadbare apron over a simple gown, and her hair had sprung loose from whatever restraints she'd imposed on it. Brown-haired and brown-eyed, she stood defiant and fearsome, for all she was a head shorter than her equally sturdy man. Pine boughs and holly decorated the mantel for the festive season. A cauldron of what looked to be some sort of porridge simmered upon the jack over a peat fire, and the sideboard held loaves of cooling bread, a dish of butter and possibly the remains of a Christmas ham. If their dwelling place needed repairs, and their clothing was worn, at least they all appeared to be eating well enough. And what a job it would be for the women and girls in this family to keep this lot fed.

The man Cruikwork hung his head and shifted, teetering.

He took a step back, and she saw the twinge of pain that spoke of more than mere wounded pride. Fitz had said Cruikwork returned from the war with a wound that continued to plague him.

She could help Fitz. She could help these people. For today, anyway.

"I'm Miss Parker." Mel skirted around the table and debris on the floor and crossed to the astonished young wife. Two doors led off this main room which seemed to be kitchen and sitting room both. She and her parents had shared a cottage like this for a short while in Portugal. She signaled to a girl of about twelve. "Fetch me a basin of hot water and a flannel, if you please. Come with me, Mrs. Cruikwork, and I'll see to your injuries."

She glanced at Fitz and felt the warmth of his regard. The young girl, however, stood frozen with her mouth agape.

"Quickly, Sarah," Fitz said. "I've sent for the midwife, Mel, but I thank you for taking charge."

She eyed the woman. "You're with child?"

"The midwife is the only medical help available right now," Fitz said.

Oh, yes. She remembered. Hermione had shared that tidbit of information.

"Cruikwork, you and I will step outside." Fitz ushered the man to the door.

"Sammy," the older woman said, "grab a broom and you and your sister clean up these broken dishes." She handed off the bigger of the two babies to an older girl and juggled the infant on her hip. "I'll just get the kettle going and fix a warm broth."

"Thank you, ma'am." Mel nudged the younger Mrs. Cruikwork, toward a door.

"Not that one." The young woman still spoke with a surly edge, but some of her steam had blown off.

A bed filled the middle of the cramped room they entered. A tall, well-polished clothes press, a washstand and mirror, and a worn armchair pressed the walls, along with a well-padded cradle. There was no fireplace or grate, and only a small window. It was a cozy squeeze for a married couple, but if they cared for each other even a little... No wonder there were so many children here.

No wonder her mother had detested that cottage in Portugal. She'd had to share a room like this with Papa.

"You will sit," Mel said.

"No, miss, I—"

"For heaven's sake. Be seated."

With a heavy sigh, Jilly lowered herself onto the chair with some grace. Was she perhaps of gentry stock, a woman who'd married down?

The young girl entered with her burdens, and Mel quickly rescued the pitcher and bowl, and took the flannel the girl had tucked under her arm.

"Will you be all right, Mama?" she asked.

Jilly clasped the girl's hand and sent her a wisp of a smile. "Yes, love."

Mel touched the water. It was merely lukewarm. Remembering the struggles to keep a good fire in the various cottages where she'd lived, she smiled at the girl and said, "well done."

"Run and help your gram with the broth," Jilly said.

With a credible curtsy, the girl scampered off, sending a long look over her shoulder before slipping out.

"She's lovely," Mel said. "Is she your eldest?"

"Yes."

She carefully wrung out the towel and dabbed at the blood drying on the woman's swelling lip. "How many children do you have?"

"Two by my first husband, Sergeant Jones, two that lived, that is, and four by Cruikwork."

"You followed the drum?"

"Yes. Jones fell at Toulouse, and then Jem took us on."

A woman alone on the Peninsula, with children? It had been a marriage of necessity likely, at least on Jilly's part. Despite their quarrels, maybe they'd grown to care for each other. Living in their current hardship would make anyone waspish. Yet Jilly hadn't barred her Jem from her bed. Perhaps it was only the more privileged classes who pushed marital separations that far. Couples like her own mother and father.

"We followed the drum for a time, my mother and I. My father was Major Parker. Mama disliked the discomfort." Though her mother had relished the attention she'd received in a world filled with so many lusty men. "We were lucky to have the means to return to England."

Jilly let out a long sigh. "'Twas in part why I married Jem. He's not a bad sort when the children behave, when his back isn't paining him, when he's not worrying himself over the roof falling in and the crops failing. 'Tis been a bad twelvemonth, and even worse since the old lord's death."

Mel's hand paused and the young woman's one good eye widened. "Not meaning to criticize the new lord."

It was said with a complete lack of conviction and a great deal of irony. The urge to jump to Fitz's defense overwhelmed her. She didn't care to hear him criticized by his tenants, no matter how much he might deserve it. "I won't tell him what you said, though even if I did, I don't believe Lord Loughton is the vindictive sort. But, Jilly—may I call you that?—do you often have disputes that require intervention by the local Justice of the Peace?"

She held her breath, wondering if Jilly would argue that Fitz wasn't the local JP.

Instead, Jilly bit her lip and tears welled in her eyes. She dipped her head. "I have a temper, miss."

A temper and the heart to admit it. Jilly was not irredeemable. "Where are your people?"

"Sussex. If you can believe it, my father was a respectable farmer. But I fell in love and ran off with a soldier. My mother is gone. A cousin holds the house and land now, and we were never close."

"There," Mel said, lifting her hand away. "You've long stopped bleeding. Shall we see about something hot to drink?"

Before she could approach the door, a small older woman entered. She set her bag on the bed, announced herself as Mrs. Astrop, the midwife, and *tsk-tsked* over the young woman's injuries. "I shall have a word with that man of yours, Jilly, and I won't be as soft as young Lord Loughton. He ought to take a horsewhip to Jem."

"I fear I hit Jem first with the fire poker."

Mel swallowed a gasp. What might he have done to deserve that?

"Even so. He's a strong man, and you're a woman. The lady here has done a fine job cleaning your wounds. Miss Parker, is it?"

"Yes. How did you know?"

"News travels fast in a village like this."

A quick knock brought the older Mrs. Cruikwork carrying a tray with two steaming bowls.

Mel's stomach fluttered.

Mrs. Cruikwork beamed a gap-toothed smile. "The neighbor just brought it. Said her son caught enough gudgeon for a good chowder to share. Though I'm guessin' she was nosin' a bit."

Fish chowder. The smell wafted up, quickly filling the small space, sending Mel's stomach from flutter to frenzy. She set her hand to her mouth and backed against the clothes press.

Jilly began a fierce gagging.

"Take that away." Mrs. Astrop aimed a finger at the door.

"Feed it to the little ones," Jilly said, catching her breath. "Go on, mam."

The midwife handed Jilly a cloth. "Come. Get yourself outside for some fresh air."

While Jilly stumbled to the door, Mel eased herself down on the chair and pulled the cloak over her nose. It smelled of horses and Fitz, and some of the nausea eased.

When she looked up, she was alone with the midwife, who was eyeing her shrewdly. "Are you all right, Miss Parker?"

Surprisingly, she had been, until the soup arrived. She waved a hand. "An aversion to fish, is all."

The older lady settled herself on the edge of the bed.

"You are engaged to his lordship, I hear."

"*Was* engaged. I've broken it off."

"Is that wise?"

"*Wise*? I beg your pardon." She didn't need to be questioned by an inquisitive midwife. Let her just catch her breath and join Jilly outside.

"I'm told that you arrived at Loughton Manor with a terrible stomach. And that you've been tossing up your food for the past couple of months."

Mel's back stiffened. "*Who told you that*?"

"I met your cousin, Lady Hermione, today when I dropped off my grandchildren for the party."

She closed her eyes and clenched her fists. Hermione had consulted the midwife about her.

Her cousin had started in October, prying, asking questions, dropping not-so-subtle hints about Mel's continued indigestion. But she hadn't known about Fitz's visits to her bedchamber at Lady Clitheroe's... they'd been discreet.

Furthermore, how could anyone possibly be certain of anything until there were definite signs? Should there be any of those, Mel wanted to be well away, shut up in her cottage in Durham. If Mother dared to venture there, she wouldn't find her until spring, and if the worst circumstances occurred, she'd at least be saved from Lord Starling's nephew, who would surely turn and run from a marriage to her.

A thin hand settled over hers. "He is a confoundedly handsome fellow, is Master Fitz. I've known him his whole life. Charming and goodhearted to boot. He deserves some happiness with a wife who'll limit herself to carrying *his* child."

Mel blinked. Had Hermione shared tales with the midwife about Mother? Mel would never play Fitz false. She would not be the cause of that sort of unhappiness.

The hand squeezed hers. "Shall I examine you?"

Mel jumped to her feet. "*Examine me*? No...Fitz...Lord Loughton... will be looking for me. I must go and join him."

"He's not here. He's taken Jem and gone off to find supplies for the roof repairs."

He'd left her alone, with the midwife paying a call. Had it been purposeful?

He deserves some happiness.

Hadn't Fitz been happy with Mary's mother?

"Now, let us start with some questions about your last courses."

No. No, absolutely, she would not be examined this day by a busybody midwife who'd known Fitz his whole life and implied things about...

"What do you mean about a wife who'll limit herself to carrying—"

"Just that is what I meant. Now, this *is* his doing, is it not? When were your last courses?"

She plopped down onto the chair, remembering.

CHAPTER TEN

Grandfather's Blessing

26 September, 1822
Lady Clitheroe's Estate, Bedfordshire

Soft tapping at her door sent her senses to full alert and she hurried to answer it.

Fitz slipped in silently, quietly closing the door and turning the key in the lock. The very air around them crackled.

"You had fair weather for your journey today," she said awkwardly.

He'd returned to Lady Clitheroe's that evening, and they'd had no more than the briefest of moments alone before announcing their engagement to their hostess and their guests.

He smiled. "You wish to discuss the weather?"

She took in a breath, shook her head, and laughed. "No." *I wish to kiss you, and more.* "Tell me what Grandfather said when he gave his blessing."

He withdrew a letter from inside his coat. "Read for yourself."

She broke the seal and scanned the few lines of the shaky hand that had become familiar to her. Grandfather's more recent letters had been written by his secretary, but often he included a postscript in his own hand. This entire note he'd written himself.

It was short and to the point. "Well then," she said.

"I take it he's not made a liar out of me? Will you share what he wrote?"

This is a good match with a sensible man, Mary Elizabeth. Don't be headstrong. Secure his hand, Granddaughter.

"He approves," she said.

"It's what he told me as well. I also received detailed instructions on the settlement agreement, which, on my honor, I will comply with."

Grandfather hadn't included those details in his note. She supposed they would be self-evident when the document was prepared.

Secure his hand.

She tossed the letter aside and went to him. His eyes glowed darkly down at her.

"Are you sure, Fitz? Any one of those young ladies downstairs—"

"I don't want them. I want *you*."

She stepped into his welcoming arms and pressed her cheek to his pounding heart. On the mantel, the candle flames flared like the spiraling warmth of her insides.

Secure his hand, Grandfather had said. She was only too willing. Yet Papa's voice whispered at her other ear: *Beware the stuffed-up lordlings, the fortune hunters, the bounders.*

Fingers swept over her cheek, moving on to burrow into her hair. Pins scattered. Fitz spun her around and completed the job, sending a cascade of tangles around her. He swept her hair aside and the next sensation was the press of his lips and the tickle of breath on her neck. Pleasure rippled through her as his warmth came around her.

And then he stepped away, leaving her shivering. He marched to the hearth and added fuel to the low fire her hostess had provided for the chilly autumn night.

"There," he said, standing and dusting his hands. "Come and sit."

Oh, he was magnificent, framed by the flickering candles and glowing fire, a bronzed god.

And he wanted *her*?

"I must ask you, Fitz. Did you request money from my Grandfather?"

"I did not. Nor did he offer any. I asked for his blessing, Mel, out of respect for him and for you. I am not as wealthy as he—nor will I be, someday, may it be many years in the future when I inherit, but you will live comfortably and well." He moved closer and took her hand. "What are your wishes for our wedding? Shall I ride to the bishop for a license, or shall we call the banns?"

When he dipped his head closer to hers, she could see a scrape near his jaw where a hasty razor had cut too close. While she was donning her night gown, he'd changed clothes and shaved. The scent of his cologne—sandalwood and oranges, subtle and manly, drew her. She set a hand to the scraped spot on his cheek. Grandfather had given his blessing. Hermione was thrilled. There was no telling what Mother would say, but she was away on the Continent. Her husband's opinion was of no account.

Secure his hand.

"By license, I think." She went to work on his neckcloth, untying and unwinding the long piece of linen. She wanted to see him again, to rake her fingers through the crisp hair on his muscled chest, but this time his whole chest and not just the bit she could see through his open shirt.

Fitz grasped her hands and raised them to his lips. "Calling the banns, and holding the wedding in either your parish or mine with family and friends present will quell gossip. Especially if we can convince your grandfather to be present."

How lovely if Grandfather would come. But not her mother. It would be dreadful to have Mother rush home from the Continent. Surely there wasn't time for her to receive news of the engagement and return by the wedding.

But what about *his* mother?

"I hope your parents will like me," she said.

"They'll adore you."

Perhaps or perhaps not. Calling the banns would give them a chance to object. It was a risk, but in all fairness, they ought to show them that sign of respect. "Very well, then. I will let you see to the banns, and we'll marry in your church."

Fitz released a long breath, the pulse in his neck bouncing. The silky belt of her robe loosened and fell, the whole garment soon falling away.

His hot hands burned through the sheer cotton nightgown, sending her blood pounding. He kissed her and need, stark and powerful, melted her insides, the warmth pooling between her legs.

He'd stirred her so, the night before, that they'd almost made love right there, in her bed. They hadn't, only because Fitz had kept his trousers on, and he'd kept his head. He'd had no qualms about giving *her* pleasure though, and she wanted more of that.

She stepped away and framed his face with her shaking hands. "Will you stay with me again tonight?"

The hands holding her waist slid up under her breasts. "I'm not sure I can hold back."

The warning stirred her more. "Then don't, Fitz. Don't hold back."

"Mel—"

"We're pledged to each other." She tugged at the drawstring of her nightgown.

His lips parted, his eyes darkened, and he watched the garment loosen and slip. Smoldering looks from suitors had always made her laugh, but this one melted her down to her toes. Still, she was an inexperienced virgin, and a giggle rose in her throat, part astonishment, part bravado. She tried to swallow it down, not wanting to scare him away.

"Mel, I—"

"You gave me more pleasure than I'd ever imagined. But you didn't take any, and I know there is more. Make me your own, Fitz."

He let out a long breath. "Are you sure?"

"Yes. Oh yes. I've waited twenty-five years for the right man."

He tugged the gown down to the tips of her breasts. The night before, he'd kissed them through the thin fabric, sending arrows of hot need down to the place between her legs, another discovery.

With another tug, the gown pooled at her hips. His hot gaze studied her breasts and his mouth parted more.

When he reached for her, she put a hand to his chest. "Now you," she said.

He grinned, and his coats and shirt disappeared.

Oh, he was magnificent. She fisted her hands to keep from touching. "Your trousers."

"Not yet." He knelt and with one tug her gown fell at her feet. Soft, warm lips touched her belly.

"Oh," she breathed as his lips moved lower. "P-please." The kisses traveled down, reaching that place between her legs that was aching with need. A large hand braced her bottom, while the other explored her inner thighs.

"The bed." She clutched his shoulders. "Stand up."

He ignored her. Or hadn't heard. Or... "Oh Fitz."

Muscles rippled under her fingers and against her bottom. Pleasure swirled and grew. Her knees wobbled, and weakened, and—

Fitz stood, juggling her. Cold air shocked the damp place where his face had been pressed. He carried her to the bed and set her down so gently she might have been floating, and then he loomed over her, his wide-eyed perusal intense, reminding her that she was naked and he...

She reached for the buttons of his trousers.

His hand swallowed hers. "Wait, Mel."

Underneath both their hands, she felt the hard length of him. She didn't want to wait.

"A moment," he whispered. "Let me drink you in, as you are."

I would like the same privilege. She was too breathless to speak the words.

The seconds ticked by. Mel held his gaze, attempting her own smoldering look, daring him. His lips quirked, he kicked off one shoe and then the other, and peeled off his trousers.

"*Oh.*" In all her years following the drum, she'd never seen this. Desire flamed in her, burning away her breath.

With a roguish grin, he eased her back. His touch was soft on her shoulders, his legs bare against hers, until they both stretched facing each other, her heart pounding out of her chest. The pad of one finger burned down her neck, over one breast and her waist and her stomach.

She copied his caress, raking the scant hair on his muscled chest, smoothing her hand down his flat stomach and...

His hand came over hers. "Not yet." He pulled her atop him and combed his fingers through her hair until it fell all around her, just as he'd done the night before. "There. I dreamed of this all day. I expected to have to wait." He lifted a strand of hair. "And I would wait, Mel. Are you sure?"

She straddled his legs and moved up. Her soft core touched his hardness and the shock of pleasure made her gasp. "Yes. Oh yes."

"Oh, my darling." Then she was on her back, his lips pressed to hers, his body pressed to hers, and she was lost.

He nudged her legs further apart and explored with his hand. "You are ready I think." His thumb stroked and his fingers probed. "Close, I think."

Pleasure came in waves, and then in an explosion that swallowed the sharp pain of his entry. And then he was filling her and moving, taking her with him over the edge again.

CHAPTER ELEVEN

Mr. Smith's Arrival

28 December, 1822
The Cruikwork Cottage, Leicestershire

"When were your last courses, Miss Parker?"

The midwife's crackly voice pulled her back from that wondrous night to the present. She searched her memory... she'd never been terribly regular, but... she could go no further back than Lady Clitheroe's house party, as if her whole life had begun there, and wasn't that just ridiculous?

"If you can tell me your last courses, this will take but a few moments."

A sharp rapping at the door saved her.

The elder Mrs. Cruikwork peeked in. "There's a servant from the manor come to fetch you, miss. Says it's urgent."

Mel jumped up. "I'll be right along. Good day to you, Mrs. Astrop."

She hurried through to the cottage kitchen, where the floor had been swept and the smaller children sat at the table spooning the vile chowder. A young groom in Loughton livery waited just inside. Holding her breath, she hurried out of the door and into the yard. Jilly was there supervising the older children as they gathered tools and ladders.

The groom handed her a note.

What could it be? No one would know to contact her here. Unless, perhaps Hermione had left word with her man of business that they'd be stopping at Loughton Manor. That was entirely possible. Perhaps there was a problem at Hermione's cottage in Hampshire. Or... Grandfather. He'd suffered a stroke some weeks ago, but his secretary had written that he was improving.

With a prayer that the news was not something too terrible, she unfolded the paper and scanned the few words.

Heart sinking, she wished for Fitz. Her grandfather's man, Mr. Smith, was waiting for her at Loughton Manor. It could only be bad news, the worst news; news that would mean an increase in her income, and leave another hole in her heart.

She steeled herself, picked her way across the yard to Jilly and asked her to let Lord Loughton know that she'd been called back to the manor on urgent business.

With the groom following, she rode along silently, grateful for the cold air stinging her cheeks while she battled her emotions. She was Major Parker's daughter and she must not cry like a ninny.

She found Mr. Smith in the parlor, warming his feet by the fire. As he stood to greet her, she spotted the black band on his arm and her knees wobbled.

"I'm very sorry to tell you, Miss Parker, Mr. Sawley has passed away."

***

"Lost part of the roof in that fierce storm last month." There was no accusation in Cruikwork's tone, nevertheless, shame rose in Fitz.

Their steward had suffered the same influenza that took father. He wasn't yet up to the task of managing Loughton Manor, and Fitz ought to have come home sooner.

Fitz walked along next to Cruikwork, who was leading the donkey pulling the laden cart. Fitz had persuaded a more prosperous tenant to part with spare wood and tiles for roof repairs, payment to be a reduction of the next quarterly rents and young Harry Cruikwork's help with the next harrowing.

"I sent word to the manor," Cruikwork said, "but her ladyship said the steward was still down with the lung fever."

And he himself had been in London when that fierce storm hit, meeting about his inheritance with solicitors, and bankers, and government functionaries. He'd also been spending plenty of hours at his club. And then there'd been a visit to Coke of Norfolk, and another party near Enderby.

"The fault is mine, Cruikwork. I should have seen to the matter. I'm sorry."

The truth was, that though he'd been seeking a way out of his problems, he'd spent much of that time in his cups.

"Besides assisting with your leaky roof, Cruikwork, how can I help make your lot easier so Jilly isn't bashing you with a fire poker?"

Cruikwork took in a deep breath and told him about one of the farms with a larger dwelling and an older tenant. The man had recently been widowed and was debating a move to Manchester to live with his only son.

Perhaps there was a way to help Cruikwork. He wasn't a layabout or a drunk. In spite of his war wounds, he worked hard. Perhaps he needed a more spacious home and a way to bring in enough money for Jilly to have an occasional new pair of gloves or a bonnet.

When they arrived at the cottage, Jilly greeted them, a sheepish expression on her battered face. "My lord, Miss Parker asked me to tell you, she's been called away."

"She's gone?" *Of course she's gone, you numbskull.* She'd been promising to leave since the moment she arrived on his front step. No matter what she said about goings on amongst her father's men and their women, no woman in her right mind with a chance at independence would want to be burdened with this lot of tenants.

"A groom came for her not long after you left."

And it had taken Cruikwork and him over an hour to wheedle the neighbor down, pack the cart, and persuade the crotchety donkey out into the snow.

"Said it was urgent."

"Go on, my lord," Jem said. "The boys'll help me get this patching done."

Jilly lifted her chin. "And I'll help."

He looked from one to the other.

"I'll keep my temper better, my lord," Jilly said.

Jem took her hand. "As will I."

The pink in Jilly's cheeks deepened. Theirs was a stormy relationship, formed out of necessity, but not lacking in real caring. Plus, there were the children they had together, and, if he was reading the signs right, another one on the way. Despite the business of the fire poker, Jem was a lucky man.

"She seemed fair worried about something," Jilly said.

It took no more persuading for Fitz to say his farewells, though his heart was heavy. Mel had seen what his life was and what hers would be, and she likely wanted nothing of these burdens. Though he couldn't imagine her ever bashing him with a fire poker over tight purse springs.

The thought made him smile and he urged his horse into a quicker pace. He wouldn't let her go without another attempt to win her back. And another after that, if need be.

CHAPTER TWELVE

Abandoned?

27 September, 1822
Lady Clitheroe's Estate, Bedfordshire

As dawn neared, Fitz crept from Mel's bed, tucked the covers around her, and hurried into his discarded clothing. When he reached his chamber, he'd only had time to shed his clothes again when a servant appeared.

He read the hastily scrawled letter and called the servant back. In moments he was dressed and striding back down the corridor to Mel's bedchamber.

Entering, he watched her a moment, dark hair spread across the pillow as she curled on her side. He touched her arm and she shot up, and then hastily pulled the covers over her naked breasts.

She squinted up at him. "You're dressed."

"I must go."

The note, written in a shaky hand, had come from Mother, and her worry had infected him with a sense of urgency.

"You're...you're leaving?"

That had come out a bit breathlessly. He sat down next to her and pulled her close. "A Loughton groom just arrived. My father is gravely ill. I must go home."

"Oh," she breathed. "Of course. Shall I follow?"

"It's the influenza. I should not like you to risk catching it."

"I see," she said, and he heard the doubt in her voice.

He swept her up against him. "I'm not abandoning you, Mel. Go home to Hampshire, and I'll make the arrangements for our wedding and come for you, as soon as father has recovered."

He felt her head move in a nod.

"This won't be a long separation. My father is a hardy man. Meanwhile, you must write to me. Will you do that?" He ran a finger over her lower lip, flummoxed to find it trembling. She was stronger than that.

"Don't worry, my love. I'll be true. You must write to me when you arrive home."

A quiver went through her. Damnation. She was going to cry.

"No tears," he pleaded. "I beg you. I'm truly not abandoning you, I promise." He thought of their love making. She'd given herself to him fully and completely, and more than once. "I'll see that the first banns are called next Sunday. If you have need of me for any reason, you must send for me immediately."

A ray of morning light caught a flash of sadness, which she quickly blinked away. "I understand. I shall pray for your father. And you." She clutched his hand. "You must stay well, Fitz."

With a kiss that was far too short, he took his leave and hurried out.

CHAPTER THIRTEEN

No More Secrets

28 December, 1822
Loughton Manor, Leicestershire

"*Everything?*" Mel squeezed her fingers against a sudden pounding in her forehead.

"Yes. Except for a few legacies to servants. Aside from the cash holdings which will come to you, you will also have the controlling shares in the bank, unless you choose to sell them."

Before his stroke, her grandfather had changed his will, leaving her almost everything. A great deal of money, certainly, but... the bank. The magnitude of the responsibility swamped her.

"But, *why?*"

She'd had a plan, and it had involved her small property in Durham and the income from her investments, the challenge of growing her nest egg, the prudence, and struggle, and work of managing it, with only herself to look out for... and Hermione too of course. Her dear cousin had only a meager income.

"Mr. Sawley was quite taken with you when you wrote and visited, and very happy when Mr. Lovelace—Lord Loughton—sought out his blessings for your betrothal."

But of course, Grandfather was pleased. It was his suggestion that they marry.

"And the sudden death of the late Lord Loughton made him sense his own mortality."

"Who did he disinherit in making this change?"

"He had planned an endowment to educate the children of the lower classes."

"Oh." A worthy cause. One she could support, if she didn't mismanage the bank and lose all the money.

How was she to *do* this?

A footman came with the tea tray and Mel swallowed a surge of nausea, her hand shaking as she poured.

But when she lifted her own cup, bile rose in her again and she pressed a napkin to her lips.

"Do excuse me a moment." She hurried to the door and pushed it open. And found Fitz, looking windblown, and concerned, and so handsome.

"Mel." He grasped her arms. "Biggs said Smith is here. Is it your grandfather?"

She nodded, fighting both the spasms in her stomach and in her heart, taking deep breaths until she could finally speak.

"He died. I must have a moment." She waved a hand. "Tea. Mr. Smith."

And then she hurried away.

She nearly collided with Lady Loughton in the hall where she was handing over the four noisy boys to the nursery maid.

"We've returned safely," Lady Loughton said. "Though everyone has had entirely too many sweets. *James, stop baiting your brother. Edward, stop whining. Everyone upstairs for your supper and we'll play games later.* Lady Hermione and the girls will arrive any moment."

All Mel could manage was a nod. She clamped a hand over her mouth and hurried up the stairs.

"Miss Parker? Are you unwell?"

Mel rushed into her bedchamber and reached the basin in time.

A soft hand touched her shoulder. "Oh, my dear." Lady Loughton's gentle tones made Mel want to melt into a puddle of tears.

Which she would not do. "My grandfather has died. His secretary is in the library with Fitz."

"Oh, no. Oh, my poor, poor dear." Lady Loughton's skirts swished and she reappeared with a glass. "Here. Take a sip of water."

Mel croaked out her thanks and let a dribble of water touch her tongue.

"My sincere condolences. Hermione told me you'd only just become acquainted with him." Her hand, smooth and cool, brushed a lock of hair from Mel's cheek. "It's very hard to lose someone we care for, and in your condition... any upset can make the nausea worse. It's dreadful, I know, casting up one's accounts at every turn, but it usually passes after a month or two, or in some cases three. Or sometimes longer. I recall that when I was carrying Fitz—"

"Oh, my lady." Cheeks flaming, Mel sank onto the edge of the bed. "What you must think of me."

She'd been as reckless as her mother. More so, when one considered that she was five-and-twenty, whereas her mother had been a mere girl of fifteen.

Lady Loughton settled next to her. "I have found the suffering to be worth it in the end. Fitz is a good man. Surely you will marry him. Do you not love my son?"

"I haven't been sure he wants me, and I won't force marriage on an unwilling m-man."

Lady Loughton studied her, her eyes filled with kindness and... sadness.

"I'm sorry." Mel wiped away a tear. "Drat it all. I'm not normally such a watering pot."

The lady smiled. "That's part of it as well. Do not you worry. I know for a fact that Fitz is not unwilling." Lady Loughton patted her hand. "You'll grow to like him one day."

"I like him now." She squeezed the older lady's hand. "I... I care for him."

Despite her doubts, that was true. When they were with one another, Fitz was kind and easy to talk to. The moment he'd stepped into Lady Clitheroe's parlor, she'd been drawn to him. He was handsome—of course there was that. But there had also been his air of vulnerability, a recent widower being chased by young magpies angling to marry him. His patient courtesy had stirred her. And still did, when she was with him. And yet... So much had happened. Could she truly trust him?

"Perhaps he told you he's made a muddle of the estate's finances, Mel—may I call you that?"

"Of course. And the finances? That is nothing." Especially now. "Did you know that he stopped answering my letters?" Her voice cracked and she swallowed hard.

At first, she'd explained away his failure to write. She'd forgiven. And then she'd felt hurt, and as she began to be sick day after day, she grew worried, and then so angry.

She cleared her throat. "But worse, is this business of neglecting the boys under his care,

Lady Glanford's boys. Will he neglect me? Will he neglect a... a child of his own?"

Lady Loughton stilled next to her for a long moment and finally spoke. "Have you asked him about these matters?"

She nodded. "He claimed he didn't receive all the letters. But regarding the neglect of his wards... he was dodging, and then we were interrupted."

Lady Loughton stood, gripping her hands in front of her, and paced to the mantel, and then back to the bed. "There's a story here that is not truly mine to tell. I don't know it all, but—"

The door opened and Fitz entered.

Mel jumped up. "I should return to Mr. Smith."

"He's just departed," He crossed the room to her. "He said he rode straight through with this news and is ready to drop. He's taken a room at the inn and will return to us tomorrow. He begged me to make his excuses."

"Of course."

Fitz took her hands. "Mother, would you allow us a private word?"

Under his kind demeanor, Fitz radiated tension. He'd heard all about her inheritance and was, perhaps, upset by it. She certainly was.

With that money, she could help him now. Would pride prevent him from accepting it? Would he be shamed by a wife who worked as a banker? Would he still want her? What was she to do?

"No, Fitz." Lady Loughton took a seat near the hearth and beckoned them. "Come, both of you, and sit. You may talk later. I have something to say before I leave."

The tone of Lady Loughton's voice, velvet over steel, startled her out of her worries.

"Very well." Fitz's lips clamped together and he followed Mel to the sofa.

Lady Loughton folded her hands together in her lap. "The news of another loved one's death makes me feel low. I confess, your father's death almost destroyed me."

"Oh, my lady" Mel said, and "Mother," Fitz said at the same time.

"No, no, grieving takes time, but I'm adjusting to being without him, day by day. Just as when we married, we had to adjust to being together, day by day. My dears, I can't let you proceed without giving you the benefit of some hard-won wisdom. You are two caring people with a chance for as much happiness as my Lord Loughton and I had. There are no guarantees, but that is part of the pleasure of plunging in with someone who you already admire. If you make the effort, you come to know each other better. You work together. You sacrifice for the other. Those things you must do, because there are always challenges—years when crops are bad, leaking roofs, troublesome children. A happy marriage requires courtesy, a willingness to forgive, and honesty. Fitz, you were discourteous to Mel, and she's not sure she can muster the willingness to forgive and commit her future to you because she has valid worries—worries that you can resolve by being honest with her. You must trust her. You must tell her about Glanford and Alice."

The long speech sent a flood of color into Fitz's cheeks. "How—"

"I love you, my darling boy. It wasn't hard to puzzle out." She stood and waved Fitz back into his seat. "Now. I shall change out of this damp gown while you two talk."

Mel studied the flames, working out what was so terribly obvious to a girl with parents like Major and Mrs. Parker. Alice was Fitz's late wife. Glanford was his friend. "They had an affair."

"Yes."

His jaw had tightened. He'd been angry about it. And humiliated most certainly. She sensed there was more.

"Tell me," she said.

"A gentleman doesn't speak ill of his wife."

If only her father and mother had shared those scruples. "For Mary's sake?"

"And because it's wrong."

"Oh. You are right. And vice-versa for a woman and her husband. I have heard that affairs are not uncommon among the aristocracy." It was also true among soldiers and their wives. "I would never want that sort of marriage for myself, going my separate way after..."

After the birth of an heir and a spare. Fitz only had Mary. His wife had died giving birth to a stillborn son. She'd violated even that society norm.

Mel clutched his hand and held it between both of hers.

"Mary's birth was so difficult that Alice and I, we lived separately, and then, a few years later she suddenly joined me in London at the very end of the Season, welcoming me into her bed. A month later, she was increasing."

"Perhaps the child was yours."

"No."

"You didn't suspect anything?"

"I was so happy she wanted another child, I believed her."

Fitz was the sort to see the best in people.

He sighed. "I didn't know until later. She'd encountered Glanford in March at a hunt. And still he had the nerve to ask for another loan that spring. Then, in the autumn he fell from his horse. I was attending his funeral when Alice went into labor, three months early, yet the child was full-term. Mrs. Astrop knew. I knew as well, when I saw him. I was wild with grief, and anger, and guilt. To my shame, I was also relieved. That child, had he lived, would have been the Loughton heir."

"You are a good man, Fitz. You would have done right by him, no matter what."

"Would I have?" He shook his head.

"Yes, you would have, hard as it might have been. Did Lady Glanford know?"

"No, and she still doesn't. I wasn't certain the child was Glanford's until after Father died. If Mother suspected, then Father knew as well. He pushed me to do more with the estate, and Mother persuaded me to let Mary continue in her care so I could go out more in society. I had no intentions of marrying again—until I met you. I love you, Mel. Can you understand? Can you forgive me?"

She thought of her mother and her many infidelities. Good heavens, if Fitz learned of those, he might worry she'd be her mother's daughter. Alice had hurt Fitz terribly. Papa had armed himself with indifference, but Mel had seen the hurt lurking beneath. She'd seen what it took for him to hold his head high and go back into battle.

"Yes. And I won't play you false, Fitz."

"Nor I you. No more secrets?"

She gulped and nodded, but her hand reflexively went to her stomach.

Fitz opened his mouth, but the door crashed open before he could speak.

"*Mel,*" Hermione cried and then spotted Fitz.

"What's wrong, Hermione?"

Her gaze skittered from Mel to Fitz and back. She bit her lip and huffed. "I cannot believe the woman. She's here."

A chill settled over Mel, and she fought a wave of panic. She couldn't face her today. Not today.

"She?" Fitz asked. "Who is *she*?"

Hermione focused on Mel, ignoring Fitz. "Neda is going to her now."

Mel leaned her head back and groaned. "My mother has tracked me down."

Hermione moved closer, wringing her hands. "It's my fault, Loughton. I wrote to Mel's mother about your engagement. I happened to mention that she'd visited Mr. Sawley. Next thing we know, a letter arrives saying to expect her by Christmas, and demanding that Mel should break with you. She'd got the harebrained idea that Sawley would leave Mel his fortune. So here Gwen comes, rushing back from France, and if I've read between the lines correctly, she's found a relation of Starling for Mel to marry." Hermione spluttered. "This will be about her wanting money. I'll go assist Neda—shall I tell Gwen you won't see her?"

It would only delay the inevitable. "No. Go and I'll join you in a moment."

"We'll *both* join you," Fitz said.

***

No more secrets. Fitz watched Mel straighten her spine and firm her jaw, as if putting on armor. He'd shared his worst secret with her, but she was, most certainly, holding back. First there was that hand to her belly, a tell-tale sign if ever there was one, especially atop all the gagging. And now this business with her mother.

The door closed on Hermione. "You're frowning," he said. "You're tense. You've gone pale. I sensed you weren't close with your mother, but you seem... fearful."

"Fearful?" She scoffed. "I'm not fearful. But she's so... *oh.*" Jaws tight, she squeezed her fists and shook one in the air. "I try to not speak ill of her, but I did so already to you, didn't I?"

He hid a smile, remembering her astonishing words. "You told me no one in their right mind would leave her a pile of money."

"Yes. The money. I never expected Grandfather would..." She choked in a breath.

"Smith told me. Slow down and breathe." He stroked her back while she gulped in more air.

"When her letter came, we decided to leave Hampshire immediately. Before that, we were going to wait until the weather cleared to travel to Durham."

"*Durham?*"

"My cottage is in Durham."

"Good God, woman, that's almost to Scotland."

"Yes, well, needs must. I assumed you no longer wanted to marry me, and I wanted to see it, and there was a good chance Mother knew nothing about it and wouldn't find me there. She's plotting. Starling has a nephew, or cousin, or some other relation who needs a rich dowry. Mother is capable of anything—I don't know what lengths she would go to. And I'm *not* going to marry him."

"You most certainly will not." *Damnation.* Mel was of age, but she was a woman with only Hermione to protect her, and if two determined men were after her, that was no protection at all. "Who is Starling?"

"Lord Starling is Mother's husband."

"Come here." He pulled her onto his lap and buried his face in her hair. She had been running away, but not from him.

Though that hand to her belly... Durham was a good distance from Hampshire. She thought he'd abandoned her, and preferred giving birth quietly in the hinterland to entering the deceptive marriage her mother was plotting. What a brave girl she was.

But... a child. *His* child. His heart took off in a brisk gallop. A brother or sister for Mary. Mel was marrying him. There'd be no question about it.

She wriggled in his arms. "We must go down and rescue your mother."

"*Shhh.*" The fire in her soft cheeks had subsided and they were dry. She hadn't cried over her grandfather yet, but that would come. "Mother is very strong. And so are you."

"After five minutes with Gwendolyn Sawley Parker Starling, she'll demand you escape such a tawdry connection. I'll understand. I don't wish the connection to my mother either." Her mouth firmed and her fists clenched again. "But, oh my God, the inheritance. What am I going to do?"

You're going to marry me, of course. "Mother won't send you away, nor will I. If you run off to Durham, I'll come after you—*you*, Mel, not your money. Regarding that, I made a promise to your grandfather and I mean to keep it. Shall we go and beard the lioness?"

"Oh Fitz." She kissed his cheek and stood. "I'll speak to her. Though when she learns of grandfather's bequest..." She rubbed at her temples. "She'll hound me until—"

"No, she won't. I'll be damned if I'll allow them to bully you."

Downstairs in the hall, the butler stood guard at the parlor door.

"How dare you, Hermione. I should like to speak to her—" The shrill voice penetrated the solid wood panels.

"*Mortifying*," Mel muttered. Color bloomed again in her cheeks, embarrassment warring with anger warring with... the fear had returned.

But she wasn't alone. She'd never be alone, not facing her mother, not facing the rest of the directors of her bank, either. He might not have a vote, but he could stand by her side.

He dropped a kiss on her forehead. "Biggs, have the visitors' carriage pulled round. They're not staying. Come, Mel. Let us see what she has to say."

CHAPTER FOURTEEN

A Previous Arrangement

The kiss gave her courage. She lifted her chin and kissed him back, full on the mouth, in front of the butler. Fitz's answering grin raised her spirits more.

Perhaps there would be hope for them. But poor Fitz—to marry a woman whose immense wealth he couldn't legally command. His wife a banker? And her mother... After what he'd been through with his first wife, would Fitz want to risk marrying the same sort of woman?

He smoothed her shoulders. "Shall we?"

"Yes." She straightened his neckcloth and tugged her shawl closer.

The corner of his mouth curved. "Girded for battle?"

She nodded, returning his smile.

Biggs opened both doors and they walked in together. Mother rose from her seat, as did her husband, the indolent Lord Theodore Starling. Another man standing near the fireplace raised a quizzing glass. She had the fleeting impression of a fellow about the same age and height and coloring as Lord Starling. Fleeting, because her mother's presence overpowered both men and dominated the room.

Blonde-haired, shapely, and still quite beautiful, Mother had only just turned one and forty, Papa having invaded the cradle to get her with child. Seeing her father in that light made Mel's heart ache. It was no wonder Grandfather had detested him.

She pulled herself together. "Lady Starling," Mel said. "Lord Starling. Such a surprise."

Mother's eyes flitted between her and Fitz, finally settling on the more interesting quarry, the handsome and virile Lord Loughton. Had Mother been single she would have vied with the girls at Lady Clitheroe's party for Fitz's attentions.

Mel's hand tightened on his arm. Mother might still chase Fitz, Lord Starling be damned. She was that sort.

She introduced her mother and stepfather to Fitz and he bowed. "Lady Starling, Lord Starling," she said, "This is Lord Loughton, my fiancé."

Fitz squeezed her hand, and beamed her a smile.

Mother's eyes blazed and her mouth tightened.

"I don't know the other gentleman, dear Fitz," Mel said.

"This is Mr. Franklin Starling," Mother said, "Lord Starling's nephew, heir to Viscount Dumphrey."

Mel dipped her head at mother's last little flourish. She was supposed to be impressed by the title.

When Fitz seated her on the sofa between his mother and Lady Hermione, she felt momentarily bereft, until Lady Loughton patted her hand.

Clever man—he was letting the Starlings know she was not alone. She had allies, two strong women, and it would look like she'd been accepted as family by Lady Loughton.

She exchanged a smile with Fitz, who took a chair nearby where he could watch her and the ladies, and all the Starlings, and more importantly, where Mel could easily see him.

"We were surprised to arrive in Hampshire and find the cottage closed up," Mother chided.

"As you have already mentioned," Hermione murmured.

"Demmed dreadful crossing," Lord Starling grumbled. "Demmed inconvenient. And expensive. Had to stay at that execrable inn waiting for Franklin to join us."

"And the matter of tracking your journey, Cousin Mary," Mr. Starling said. "And finding you *here*." He frowned at Mother. Perhaps he was a victim in all of this as well.

Mother cleared her throat. "Yes, and I must speak candidly, Mary Elizabeth. Though I can see that Lord Loughton is quite...desirable..." She batted her eyelashes. "I was shocked to learn of your sudden engagement and plans to marry so quickly after his first wife's demise."

Oh, that was rich. She exchanged a look with Fitz. Had she told him about mother's hasty marriage to her lover after Father's death? She couldn't remember.

"Really, Gwen? A quick marriage after a spouse's demise?"

Mother ignored Hermione's sarcastic mutter and went on. "So quickly after an acquaintance of mere days? It was fortunate the nuptials were delayed." She paused for a dramatic breath.

Fortunate? Lady Loughton's husband, Fitz's father, had fallen terribly ill and died.

Mel's eyes met Lady Loughton's and she saw the flare of emotion there. "I'm sorry," she said.

Lady Loughton took Mel's hand and held it between both of hers. Mother's gaze fixed on the move and her frown deepened.

"Mary Elizabeth, your stepfather and I have not given our approval to this marriage. You must know, Lord Loughton, a previous arrangement was made. Mary Elizabeth was promised to Mr. Franklin Starling."

"Is that so?" Fitz drawled. "I understood that Miss Parker is of age and can decide for herself."

"I am. I haven't seen any marriage agreements, much less signed one, nor was I privy to any such arrangements. Promised by whom, Mother?"

"Why, it was arranged when Major Parker died."

"Arranged by whom? Certainly not by my dear papa."

"By your stepfather and me. Why, who else has a say over a daughter's future?" She cocked her head and leaned in. "Hermione wrote that you have struck up a correspondence with your grandfather. Surely *he* has not taken an interest in you?"

"We did not tell her yet." Hermione's stage whisper carried throughout the room.

"You've heard the news?" Mel whispered back.

Hermione nodded.

"Tell me what?" Mother's voice crackled with strong emotion. "What news?"

Mel eased in a breath, quelling a new wave of anger for the grandfather and father who, despite their own flaws, had been so ill-used. Lady

Loughton slipped a hand free and settled it on Mel's back.

"Grandfather has died."

Mother's eyes widened and she blinked, reaching for her handkerchief, and drumming up tears. Crying at will was one of her talents.

Lord Starling cleared his throat. "And what of his estate?"

***

Fitz's knuckles whitened around the arms of his chair. The blackguard. Starling—more like Vulture—was younger than Mel's mother, perhaps the same age as the man he called his nephew. Perhaps younger than himself even. He'd probably never bothered to attempt an acquaintance with his bride's father.

Color flooded Mel's cheeks and then drained, and her lips quivered with the shakiness that came over her when she was about to be ill.

He pushed out of his chair. They were finished with this group of predators. "Miss Parker will send you the name and direction of Mr. Sawley's solicitor so you may make inquiries." He nodded to her encouragingly, watching her gather her composure.

"Most certainly, I will," she said. "Leave word with Lord Loughton's butler where you may be contacted."

Hermione and his mother stood, raising Mel up between them.

She *was* ill. He needed to shuffle these bloody vipers away.

"You will want to rest from your journey," Mother said. "You will find the Royal Swan to be a very comfortable and respectable inn, one of the best in England."

Starling was enough of a gentleman to rise with the ladies, but Mel's mother remained firmly seated, even sliding back further upon her chair. "We have not finished here. You are not free to marry Lord Loughton. Especially now, so soon after your grandfather's death, with the estate to be settled. I must firmly object. We must object, Lord Starling and I."

"Duly noted," Fitz said. There were no legal grounds for an objection. Mel was of age when her father died, and she claimed to know nothing about a contract. The banns were properly posted and the vicar had the living on the Loughton estate.

Still, given enough time, Mel's mother might throw up an objection the Church would feel obligated to consider.

While his mother and Hermione moved toward the door, Fitz tucked Mel's frigid hand over his arm. "I am sure that Miss Parker will give as much consideration to your feelings as you have given to hers and those of the late Major Parker. Mr. Sawley's feelings will be evident to you in his will once that is revealed. Now, I must speak candidly as well. You must be on your way. The ladies have had a tiring day with the children."

"I could use a pint now," Mr. Starling muttered.

Mel's mother's lips firmed. "Before I leave, Mary Elizabeth, I would hear your promise that you won't marry."

Mel scoffed and opened her mouth to speak.

"*Give it back.*" Maniacal laughter flowed through the open parlor doors along with the sound of pounding feet. James burst into the room, the three younger boys in pursuit. At the sight of the visitors, James froze, but the other three saw only their prey. They pounced, and all four boys collapsed onto the carpet in a giggling, raucous, free-for-all.

Next to him, Mel had begun trembling, one hand over her mouth. She caught his eye, and he saw she was laughing.

Mel's mother spluttered and waved a hand. "Why I...Aren't you going to *stop* them?"

"Boys." Mother shook her head. "I have six of them, Lady Starling. Sometimes it's better to let them settle on their own."

Fitz beckoned Biggs and the two sturdy footmen who'd joined him in the hall.

"Shall we break them up, my lord?"

"Best give those three a moment to set James straight. I'm sure he's done something to deserve this. The visitors are leaving now. Please escort them out to their carriage."

"Tossed out," Mr. Starling muttered. "Good work, Gwen."

With a huff, Mel's mother finally stood. Soon enough they'd closed the door on the family of Starlings, and Fitz went to sort out the tangle of boys.

***

"I am so very sorry." Mel wiped a tear that had come from laughing so hard. *Good Lord, Mother's face.* "My mother is the sort to push and prod, and unsettle the world around her until she gets exactly what she wants. I thought she'd never leave."

"We had to unleash our secret weapon." Fitz's smile warmed her down to her toes, making her laugh again.

"Wild little brothers and their friends."

"The Glanford boys will be family soon. James and Edward are gloating about being their uncles."

"Can you truly tolerate the connection to my mother?" If not, perhaps Mr. Smith would escort Mel to Grandfather's estate in Bedfordshire.

Her hand went to her stomach. No, Bedfordshire might be out of the question for the next several months.

She glanced at Fitz and found him watching her. Oh, Jupiter, she was being ridiculous. Fitz had risen to her defense, as had his mother. And she could help them and the tenants now that she was Grandfather's heir.

The thought of the money... the bank... the responsibility... The carpet rippled beneath her.

Her feet left the floor. With a great rustling of skirts Fitz deposited her back on the sofa where she'd sat confronting her mother, her head now cradled against his shoulder. She inhaled the comforting scent of fresh air, starch, and horse, and the undefinable musk she recognized as his.

He slipped away and moments later pressed a tumbler into her hands. "Brandy," he said. "Drink."

She peered at him over the glass. "People are always handing me drinks, as if I'm some addlepate."

"Or perhaps a ninnyhammer."

She laughed, swallowed and choked. Fitz patted her on the back until she'd finished coughing.

"I never did acquire a taste for spirits."

"One more sip," he said. "Slowly this time."

She complied, and set the glass aside. "I ought to have told you more about my mother. She was already living with Starling while Father was dying. She came for Papa's funeral, and then returned to Kent and married him almost immediately. But before that, she was unfaithful. Often. With many different men. I ought to have told you."

"Your grandfather hinted at that when I asked for your hand."

"He knew?"

"He kept abreast of her whereabouts and activities through the years."

"Perhaps he meant to leave her something if he found that she'd changed."

He shrugged. "What about your father? Was he faithful to her?"

Oh Papa. "I always forgave him because of what he put up with. Fitz, I won't have that sort of marriage—arguing, going off with other lovers, living in the same home like strangers. I swore I'd never be as impetuous as them. But here I am."

***

Fitz put aside his brandy and leaned close. Mel had set her hand to her waist again in that same protective gesture. "You said your father and mother anticipated their vows." *As we did?*

She raised an eyebrow, and he wanted to laugh, but instead he reached for her. He *was* an idiot. It had taken months and months before Alice conceived Mary. The thought that Mel might be with child hadn't crossed his mind when he was swanning about London and visiting country houses. "I *know*," he whispered.

A frown furrowed her brow. "Your mother, Hermione, Mrs. Astrop, all think I'm increasing. How can anyone possibly know? How do they know? How do you know?"

"I'm the eldest of ten." He ought to have been an accoucheur, he was that good at spotting the signs that a new sibling was coming.

"Did everyone know but me?"

"You were in denial, Mel. In your heart, you knew. That's why you allowed yourself to be led to Loughton Manor."

She scoffed. "I didn't..." Color rose in her cheeks and her lips quirked. "When did *you* know?"

"The day you arrived here, I suspected. The next morning when you picked at your breakfast, I was almost certain. We'll know for sure when the baby quickens in the next month or so." He traced a finger over her full breasts, down her bodice to the swell of her abdomen. "I should examine you now and give a more informed diagnosis."

She huffed and laughed but the shiver that went through her raised his spirits. He touched his lips to hers, relishing the softness and the way she opened her mouth to welcome him.

"What say you?" He murmured against her lips. "Are you too great now to be tied to a bumbling baron who's only argument is that he loves you and doesn't want to live without you?"

Soft fingers stroked his jaw. "Oh, Fitz. You're not a bumbler. You're quite wonderful, actually. I ought to have done more than write to you. I ought to have come after you. I was being a coward, and then when my mother's letter arrived, I decided to run. It's what Papa used to do when Mama... when he'd had enough of her, and when she was unfaithful."

"I wasn't unfaithful to you." He swiped a hand over his face thinking about his first marriage. During the long separation, he'd always been discreet, but not always faithful. "With Alice, I wasn't always—"

"No." Mel set a finger over his lips. "That is the past. I'm neither my mother, nor Alice. I'll be true to you."

"And I to you."

She offered her hand. "We must shake on it."

Her smile reminded him of the evening they spent at the inn. He took her hand, flipped it over and touched his lips to her palm, so warm and soft. The other warm and soft parts of her beckoned, and he would uncover them that very night, but first they must settle things.

"When shall we marry? Your mother and her husband had no right to sign a contract on your behalf. Any lawsuit for breach of promise will be between them and the nephew."

"And if she rushes into church to object?"

The mantel clock chimed and he glanced out the window. Darkness had settled on Leicestershire. "Is your mother the sort to attend morning services?"

"Only if the vicar is virile and handsome."

He laughed, thinking of the elderly man who'd served their parish for so many years. "Good. I'll hie to the vicar's and interrupt his dinner."

"Papa?"

Mel peered around him and smiled. "Mary?"

His little girl stood in the doorway, clutching a book.

"Come, my darling." Fitz beckoned and she crossed the room. He pulled her onto his lap, and inhaled her sweet scent. "What's afoot, lambkin?"

"Grandmama is cross with us. She promised a scavenger hunt tonight, but the boys ruined things and now we must put it off until tomorrow." She wrinkled her brow. "I heard a lady shouting."

Fitz glanced at Mel. She bit her lip and said, "That was my mother."

"Why? Did you spill something on her gown or interrupt her when she had company? My mama used to get angry when I did that."

"She was unhappy with me."

"But why?"

He could see that Mel was searching for how to answer. His girl could be a relentless inquisitor.

"Mary, my darling girl," he said. "I've asked Miss Parker to be my wife."

"You did that months ago, Papa."

Fitz laughed and touched her nose. "You knew?"

"Of course. Miss Parker, don't you want to marry my papa?"

Mel nodded. "I do."

"Why is it taking so long? Is it b-because of me?"

The quiver in her voice pricked at his guilt. He'd neglected Mary as well.

"Not at all." Mel reached out, and when Mary went willingly onto her lap his heart swelled. Mel would make a caring mother.

She brushed a lock of hair back from Mary's face. "I'm delighted with you and so happy I'll be your mama."

"Will you shout at me like your mother shouted at you?"

"I will certainly shout if you are about to fall into the fire or the brook, or encounter some other danger, and maybe, on very, very rare occasions when I am very tired or very cross and you misbehave." Her pause, and the wink she sent Fitz made him swallow a laugh. "But you must tell me, do you misbehave often?"

"Hardly ever." She handed Mel her book. "Will you read me a story?"

"Mary." Mel tucked the book under her arm. "Is there perhaps a nursery maid looking for you?"

Mary lifted a shoulder.

"Well then. Your papa has an errand to attend to, and I will escort you upstairs and we'll let the maid know you've been found. Will you give me a tour of the nursery? I haven't seen it yet. And then I'll read you one story."

Fitz plucked Mary from Mel's lap and set her on her feet, then dropped a quick kiss on Mel's lips and Mary's head. "I'll stop at the Swan and rescue Smith from the Starlings. Please ask Turner to ready a bedchamber for him. And Mel?"

"Yes?"

"*Do* wait up for me."

Color flooded her cheeks as she nodded.

Mary tugged her hand. "Why not two stories?"

When Mel sent him a smile over her shoulder, Fitz laughed out loud.

CHAPTER FIFTEEN

A Wedding Breakfast

29 December, 1822

In spite of the chill that December morning, parishioners lingered outside offering well-wishes to Lord Loughton and his new lady.

"You've surprised us all, miss—I mean, my lady," Jilly Cruikwork said. All the members of the Cruikwork family had been in attendance.

"Apologies for the trouble yesterday," Jem said. "I'd no idea today was to be your wedding."

Mel shared a smile with Fitz. The banns were not yet void, and the vicar had been only too happy to marry them, and with her mother and Lord Starling still tucked away at the Royal Swan, when the Vicar asked for objections, no one spoke up.

"We decided there should be no more delays," Fitz said.

Jilly and Jem shared a smile and wished them much happiness.

After accepting more congratulations and good wishes, Fitz escorted Mel to the Royal Swan, where the landlord welcomed them into a private dining room, and sent a maid off with a note inviting the Starlings to breakfast with them.

Fitz had visited the inn the night before, returning to Loughton Manor with a hastily dressed Mr. Smith. Lord and Lady Starling had fortunately retired early to their rooms. Fitz said that while Smith was packing his things, he'd encountered Mr. Franklin Starling in the tap room. Mr. Starling claimed he'd been misled about Mel's interest in marrying him. He'd bought Fitz a pint and declared his intention to depart at first light.

When Fitz and Mr. Smith returned, there'd been no time for romance, only practicalities that stretched to the wee hours, preparing their marriage agreement and planning this morning's meeting at the Royal Swan.

They were on their second pot of tea when their guests appeared.

"What is this?" Mother said. "What are you up to, Mary Elizabeth?"

Her insides quivered, as they always did when she was dealing with Mother. Surprisingly though, this wasn't the morning sickness. That hadn't troubled her at all this day.

Fitz squeezed her hand, encouragingly. "Mel has something to tell you."

The serving girl appeared with a tray, and they waited as she set out dishes of bacon, sausage, eggs, and breads, as well as a fresh pot of tea and another of coffee. Not that she'd be able to eat anything now that Mother was here.

When the door closed on the servant, Mel glanced at Fitz again. He nodded.

"Lord Loughton and I were married this morning."

Mother shot out of her seat. "*No*. You're to marry Franklin."

Lord Starling looked up from his sausages. "Franklin's out of it, Gwen. Left me a note. Departed this morning for London."

Mother's eyes darted around the room and then settled on Mel in a challenging glare that soon softened into a wheedling pout.

Over and over, her mother had plied her wiles, bullying and then pleading; nagging, and then begging. She'd run off, and come back, and then expect to be treated with love and sympathy and a respect that she'd never earned.

Fitz squeezed her hand again, reminding her she wasn't alone. "How much, Mother?"

Mother's expressive face went through another series of changes. Confusion gave way to astonishment, then to understanding, and then to the sharp glint of greed. "He left you his money."

Starling's hands stilled around his knife and fork.

Mother beamed a seductive smile at Fitz. "You were a wealthy man before, Lord Loughton, but now you're as rich as Croesus. I wondered how my plain daughter snared you."

"Plain? Forgive me, but your vision must be failing. My bride is beautiful, inside and out, and very wise." He reached into his coat and pulled out an envelope. "Shall I, my love?"

Their plan to dispose of the Starlings included allowing them to believe Fitz had control, yet he offered her this display of respect.

Heart swelling, she smiled. "Yes please, Fitz."

Fitz passed the envelope to Starling. When Mother snatched it from his hand, Starling shrugged and went back to sawing his sausages.

Hands shaking, Mother unfolded the document and read, a small smile quickly squashed. "This won't cover half my debts."

As Fitz had said, Grandfather had kept himself informed. "It will cover your debts twice over, and the income will add to what Papa left as your dower. You may leave Starling when you're bored with him and still live quite comfortably."

Mother's hand hit the table, rattling the dishes. "It's not fair. I was his daughter, and he never gave me anything."

"I was *your* daughter, and you never gave *me* anything."

Fitz pushed back his chair and stood, drawing her up with him. "If you decide to sign the document, leave it with the innkeeper," he said, all disarming affability. "He'll see that Mr. Sawley's man gets it and then your creditors will be paid and the income disbursed."

Mel took his arm. "Goodbye. Safe journeys."

While Mother spluttered, Mel kept her touch on Fitz's arm light and refused to look back. By the time they reached their carriage, she was shaking.

He handed her in and drew her into his arms. "You did very well, Lady Loughton. I imagine this interview was far more unpleasant than anything you'll face with the bank's board members."

"Do you think so? Oh, you must be right. I hope we are finished with her. I hope Starling keeps her. I dread the thought of her turning up on your doorstep."

"On *our* doorstep. And we'll let tomorrow see to tomorrow." He pulled her onto his lap. "I intend to see to today, Lady Loughton."

***

Fitz's mother's plans for the celebration of their nuptials had included not just a wedding breakfast but a hastily organized celebration with neighbors, tenants and their families, one that included a rousing game of Snapdragon. It seemed forever before they closed the door on the last guest and Mel and Fitz tucked Mary into bed.

"I fear she'll expect us both to attend her every night from now on," he said, leading Mel out of the nursery and down the stairs.

"Well, what else shall we do at night?" she teased.

He paused on the landing just under the mistletoe. "Minx. This, for starters." He kissed her thoroughly, making her insides melt in anticipation, and then hurried her along the corridor—to *his* bedchamber.

"Your mother said Maggie would be waiting for me next door."

"You don't need a maid." He turned her around and went to work on her hooks. "You have me."

The dress fell about her and she stepped out of it and into his arms.

"Now and forever, Mel."

"Yes," she said. "Oh yes."

December, 1823
Loughton Manor, Leicestershire

Crooning a lullaby he'd sung to Mary when she was a babe, Fitz held the six-month-old to his shoulder while pacing the floor.

The door opened with a waft of cool air that stirred the candleflame, and Mel slipped in. "Asleep?" she whispered. She angled her head as he turned and smiled. "Yes."

Fitz set the small body in the bassinette and straightened the light blanket. "And Mary?"

"After three stories, I tucked her in and left, with strict orders she was not to join the boys in a biscuit raid."

"Are we raising a hoyden?"

"Most certainly. In a few years, she'll be leading all the little boys into mischief."

The Lovelace sons had finally produced their own boys—Rupert's and Selwyn's boys in the spring, and George's boy in September.

But this boy in the bassinette, Henry Gregory Parker Lovelace, would be the heir. Their son. Poor lad. It was good he had a clever mother.

He pulled Mel into his arms. "We'd best lock the door."

Her low chuckle heated him to his soles and he had no thought for anyone but his brilliant, impossible, impetuous bride.

The End

A Note from the Author

I hope you've enjoyed Mel and Fitz's story, Book 3 in my Upstart Christmas Brides Series!

Fitz first appeared as the "villain" of sorts in Book 2, *Convincing the Countess*, as the brother of that story's hero, George Lovelace. George, in turn, first appeared as a secondary character (another "villain"!) in *The Duke She Despised* Book 1 of the series.

Research for this story had me looking into the world of Regency banking and investing, a fascinating subject. There were, in fact, many banks during the period that were owned or co-owned by women. The real-life Lady Jersey became fabulously wealthy when she inherited an interest in her grandfather's bank.

As usual, my characters and story are entirely fictional, and any historical errors are mine alone.

Many thanks go to editor Tessa Shapcott, and as ever, I'm grateful to my late husband for his unfailing encouragement and support during the writing of this story.

I love hearing from readers! Please follow me on Facebook, Bookbub, Pinterest, and at my website, AlinaKField.com. And for monthly news about releases and sales, sign up for my newsletter at my website. I promise I won't spam you or sell your email address!

Best regards and happy reading!

Alina K. Field

Books by Alina K. Field

Sons of the Spy Lord Series

Marrying Mr. Gibson

Previously titled *The Bastard's Iberian Bride*

Paulette Heardwyn rushes to visit her dying
guardian, set on learning the truth about her
father. But the only man with answers takes his
secrets to the grave, leaving her penniless—
unless she marries his illegitimate son

The Viscount's Seduction

Lady Sirena Hollister has lost everything, even
her fey abilities. But when the fairies hand her a
chance at a London Season, her schemes for
revenge stir up an unknown enemy, and spark
danger of a different sort, in the person of a
handsome Viscount.

The Rogue's Last Scandal

Falling—literally—into the arms of the *ton*'s most
outrageous rogue seems a risky path of escape,
but Maria Graciela Kingsley y Romero has no
other choice. Only England's greatest spy lord
can help her, and he is not to be found—so his
son will have to do!

The Counterfeit Lady

Vowing she'll never submit to an arranged marriage, an earl's daughter bolts for the seaside cottage that will someday be hers. But she finds her quiet refuge occupied by the last man she ever wants to see—an American artist, who's also a thief. And, quite possibly one of her father's spies.

Avenging the Earl's Lady

The long war is over, but honor requires vanquishing one last enemy, and the Earl of Shaldon has no time for romance. But when the lady he longs for interferes in his plot, and his enemy strikes at her, nothing else matters but avenging his lady.

Novellas and Holiday Stories

The Marquess and the Midwife

A Christmas Novella
Finalist, 2016 National Reader's Choice Award

Uncovering a lie drives a new marquess back from a self-imposed exile at Christmas to find the only woman he's ever loved. Finding her turns out to be easy, uncovering her stunning secrets, a bit harder. But winning her back will be the greatest challenge of all.

A Leap Into Love

A Sweet Regence Romance Novella, a sequel to
The Marquess and the Midwife

Can a gentleman be too charming?
The ladies of Upper Upton think so.
When the single ladies of the village conspire to teach their
charmer a lesson that might bankrupt him, the town's
loveliest young widow—who's sworn off marriage forever—
steps up to warn him.

Liliana's Letter
Finalist, 2015 National Reader's Choice Award

The Matchmaker Meets the Matchbreaker

Liliana Ashford's future as a professional chaperone
depends on her wealthy charge's successful marriage, but
her own close encounter with a scoundrel years ago makes
her determined to save the girl from the same kind of rogue.

The Ghost of Depford Hall
A short, sweet Halloween story, a sequel to
Liliana's Letter

It's her mother's last All Hallows' Eve.
When family, friends, and tenants gather,
goblins, ghouls, and ghosts are banned from this
All Hallows' Eve party.
Only, no one told the Ghost of Depford Hall!

Courted by the Earl
Previously titled *Bella's Band*
A 2015 RONE Award Finalist

Saddled with his brother's title and debts,
nothing about this new life makes the Earl of
Hackwell want to stay—until he meets a lady
with a secret that can change everything.

Rosalyn's Ring

2014 Book Buyer's Best Winner, Novella Category

Done with grieving her losses, a late nobleman's daughter has fallen into a tidy spinster's life in London. But when one snowy Christmas Eve, a young woman needs rescue, she seizes the chance to do good—and to recover a family heirloom that ought to be hers.

Haunting Miss Fenwick

Thrilled to finally have a permanent home, a Squire's daughter won't let a supernatural creature scare her away. While hunting the ghost she doesn't believe in, she stumbles upon a mysterious flesh and blood man who might be the key to all of her problems.

The Upstart Christmas Brides

The Duke She Despised

Hiding her true identity, a young vicar's widow takes a position as housekeeper in a remote Scottish castle at Christmas for a new duke who years ago sabotaged her chance for happiness. She quickly falls for the duke's charming but not very competent factor, not knowing that he's hiding something also—he's the duke she despised!

Convincing the Countess

When a business-minded aristocrat encounters a
fetching widow he knew years earlier as the bride
of a ne'er-do-well earl, temptation steers him
along a track that may derail all his plans. Can he
convince her to set a course for her future that
includes him?

The Impetuous Heiress

Before dashing Lord Loughton can make amends
with his neglected fiancée, the lady's meddling
cousin delivers her to his doorstep. He soon realizes more is amiss than his carelessness. Can he
uncover her secrets and win her back before he
loses her altogether?

The Macbeth Series

Fated Hearts,
A Love After All Retelling of the Scottish Play

A Scottish Baron returning from two decades at
war meets the wife he divorced and the daughter
he disavowed before she was born, only to learn
that everything he'd believed was a lie. Determined to win back the only woman he's ever
loved he must first face the viper who drove them
apart.

The Comtesse of Midnight

A Scottish Earl on a quest for the elusive Comtesse de Fontenay, rescues a French lady smuggler during a devastating storm, taking shelter with her. As the stormy night drags on, he suspects she knows the lady he's seeking, the lady who holds the secret to his identity.

Claims of the Heart

Since a perilous fall, Lucie Macbeth has been seeing more than a settled future as the heiress to a Scottish barony. The visions plaguing her include a man—one far above her class and breeding, and English to boot. He's engaged to a duke's granddaughter as well, and thus wholly inappropriate. Though she can't marry him, and she won't become any man's leman, when the Sight warns her of danger to him her conscience, and her heart tell her she can't walk away.

Find out more at
https://AlinaKField.com
and sign up for my monthly emails for news about upcoming books and sales.

An Excerpt from
The Duke She Despised

"Well, I've done it, George. I've dismissed the bastard."

Andrew MacDonal, new Duke of Kinmarty, tugged at his neckcloth, tearing off the constricting cloth and tossing it aside.

His friend, the Honorable George Lovelace, handed him a glass of brandy, and raised his own in salute. "And just how bad are things, your grace?"

Andrew waved a hand at a desk scattered with ledgers. "Look for yourself. And cease with the 'your-gracing'. Would that I was still plain Mr. Andrew MacDonal, enjoying my spartan bachelor rooms."

George settled into the massive desk chair and moved the lamp closer.

Andrew poured himself another drink. "I'd hoped to leave before Hogmanay. But looking at those ledgers, looking at the condition of this old heap and the village—I'm guessing Kinmarty has had a rough go under Haskill's stewardship."

He should have been here to help the old duke. Why hadn't he come?

Because he'd been too angry, too selfish, too utterly bereft after Evan's departure for India. He'd filled his time with every jolly manly pursuit he could drum up—cards, women, drink, and pretended it was enough. And now he was truly, totally, completely bereft. Now he had no one at all, except the multitude of mouths dependent upon him.

"I'll stay at least through Hogmanay and give the tenants a proper New Year's celebration." They'd have a grand bonfire, one that would honor the old duke and the duke who should have been, his brother, Evan. "Then I'll find a competent factor to help sort out this tangle, and I'll go south to see about finding money."

Would that he could go back to his old life and wake up from this nightmare that had started with news of Evan's death.

George opened a ledger. "You'll be required to put on your robes and coronet and take your seat in the Lords."

"Those fusty Scots nobles never cast a vote for Old Horace. Neither will they elect me to represent them in Lords." Dear God, he hoped not.

"And then there's the matter of an heir. You'll need a proper wife for that. Preferably one with a fat dowry."

"Bite your tongue."

George smirked. "There'll be plenty of stuffed purses willing to dangle their daughters for the title of duchess. And you're a handsome devil, so the ladies of London tell me."

"I was better off being an untitled devil." He waved toward the books again. "So, what do you think?"

George and his brother were crack managers of their father's wealth. George would have spotted in five minutes what had taken himself half the day to uncover.

"If it was only a factor you wanted, you might have left the old one in place. There isn't much more for him to embezzle."

"Bloody thief. How old Horace didn't catch him...tight as a drum, the man was..."

George traced down a column of figures. "He'd been ill, you said."

"Aye. I suppose that was it." Old Horace had been a skinflint to beat them all. Looking at the books, he understood why. Poor rents, poor crops, and a village populated with shoy-hoys only fit to scare away birds.

He swiped a hand through his hair and went to throw on another one of the logs they'd scrounged, moving by rote. "Good of you to come along and offer moral support, George."

George had been with him when the letter dooming him arrived. They'd been hoisting toasts to Old Horace upon his passing, and to the new duke, his brother Evan. He'd been drowning his guilt over his neglect of the old man and rejoicing that Evan would have to return from India. Then he and his brother could reconcile. He'd do whatever it took to make peace. He wanted his brother back.

The letter had dashed all his hopes.

He poured another brandy, trying to shake the bleak memories.

"Shall you call in the magistrate?"

"No. Haskill can claim the old duke knew all and approved. Or claim his own incompetence."

"At least send an express to the bank and the solicitor letting them know what you've found. You might also reconsider your order to cancel the hiring of the housekeeper and butler. If you decide you must let the Castle, it might be more appealing to have staff in place. Not to mention, there's much upkeep needed before you even consider offering it."

"I'll winkle out the old butler. He retired hereabouts. He might know of a competent replacement for Haskill."

If he could convince the old butler, Forbes, to help him. His hand shook around the glass, and this time the brandy soured his stomach.

He was hungry, was all.

"What are we to eat *tonight*, George? I'm afraid my skills go no further than toasting some of that stale bread from the larder. You did far better with the eggs you discovered. For two farthings, I'd hand you this whole bloody dukedom and let *you* play cook, factor, and lord of the manor all in one."

"Tut-tut. No self-pity, not with so many prime acres for stalking."

Andrew glanced toward the window. Outside, thick snowflakes danced in the waning light. "And I shall grant you that stalking I promised, if you don't mind being knee-deep in snow."

A faint pounding started up. Andrew rubbed at his temple. "Another one of the bloody banging shutters that kept me up all night, do you suppose? Or might that be one of the legendary ghosts?"

George raised an eyebrow. "Or might it be someone at the door?"

Andrew tilted his head to listen, bile rising in him. "I locked Haskill out not a quarter of an hour ago and barred the door. Did the bastard forget something?" He looked around for his castoff neck cloth.

Never mind. If this was Haskill at the door, he wouldn't risk bloodying the thing when he kicked the man out on his arse again.

Cold air overwhelmed him in the hall, the sort of damp chill oozed by a medieval pile left unheated for years.

He wished for his overcoat, flung over a chair in the study, since neither he nor George had brought so much as a groom.

They'd tended their horses themselves as well, and washed in the ice-cold buckets they'd had to carry up. George, though, had managed a shave and fresh linens, the pompous ass.

George wasn't the one who'd been plunged into despair. George hadn't just been encumbered with a crumbling castle and a bankrupt estate. George hadn't just learned he'd lost his only brother months and months earlier to a fever.

Andrew rubbed at his chin. No neckcloth and two days-worth of beard—this had better not be a social caller.

He unbarred the door and yanked the heavy wood open.

In the half-light a woman stood, ramrod straight despite her shivering, swathed in dark wool.

"I beg your pardon," she said. "I knocked at the servants' door but no one answered."

By God, she was an Englishwoman, and she didn't speak like a servant.

Her wrap slipped, and he peered closer, his interest stirring. She was youngish, and from what he could see, attractive.

"I'm the new housekeeper."

A blur of dark fur shot through the door and they both jumped.

"I believe that was a cat." She peered around him.

"I've never seen it before." The bloody thing scurried off toward the bowels of the Castle and out of sight.

"May I come in?" She cleared her throat. *"No one is answering the servants' door."*

A sharp gust of wind blasted him. He apologized, stepping back, watching her enter.

The heavy wrap outlined a shapely woman. She put him in mind of Mrs. Ramsey, Old Horace's faithful housekeeper for so many years. 'Twas whispered that she had been more than a servant, and perhaps it was true given the old man's sharp decline after her death.

The new housekeeper placed a valise and a basket on the black and white tile.

"Are these all your belongings, or have you left a driver out in the snow?"

"I walked and—"

"Walked? In this weather?" Either she was of hardy stock, or he'd soon have to call the apothecary to treat her.

"Yes," she said. "I've a trunk at the inn, to be brought up when the weather eases."

He scoffed. "Next spring, then, perhaps."

She sent him an arch look and slipped the shawl back from her head, taking a bonnet with it and revealing errant dark locks that curled about her cheeks and dangled on her shoulder.

Her attention traveled over the dark paneling and up to the painted cornice with its scenes of medieval knights and their ladies. She gasped. "It's astonishing. Like...like a fairy tale castle."

A fairy tale castle? Was she mad?

The scenes might have once fascinated his childish heart, but he'd outgrown such nonsense.

She leveled a gaze at him. "What is your name, young man?"

His name? He blinked. *Young man?* He was likely older than her.

A chuckle bubbled up, the first moment of lightness he'd experienced in days. She thought he was a servant. A servant in a fairy tale castle.

Well, well. How would a lackey behave toward an arriving housekeeper?

"Never mind." She reached for her basket. "Just show me the way to the servants'—"

He snatched up the hamper. The aroma of stewed meat escaped from under the heavy cloth, making his mouth water. "You must first be introduced. Come along. The duke conducts business in the study."

Her hand went to her disheveled hair. "I must—"

"You are fine as you are." As he nudged her along, a beam of light caught her features.

His prickle of interest bloomed into full-fledged awareness. Full lips, porcelain skin, and a determined little chin—his new housekeeper was more than fine, and she spoke like a Mayfair matron. A youngish one. The urge to become better acquainted overwhelmed him.

Except, he was a duke now. Blast it. Why did Evan have to die and leave him this burden?

He reached up to tug his neckcloth and found it missing. Her frown showed she'd noticed, and that made him smile again.

"No one expected a bonny housekeeper."

Dark eyes glinted at his impertinence.

So much for the letter he'd sent to cancel her hiring. He was keeping her, at least through Hogmanay.

The Duke She Despised is available at all major booksellers.

www.ingramcontent.com/pod-product-compliance
Lightning Source LLC
Chambersburg PA
CBHW051252170626
46809CB00004B/1608